House of Glass

BOOK 2: THE EXODUS SERIES

By Austine Etcheverry
&
D. Jean Quarles

Published by Rocky Mountain Creative Publishers
707 Park St., Apt 1, Alexandria, MN 56308
www.rockymountaincreativepublishers.com
(A division of Rocky Mountain Entertainment)

First published in 2013
Copyright © 2013 by Austine Etcheverry & D. Jean Quarles
All rights reserved.

The Library of Congress Cataloging-in-Publication Data
is available from the Library of Congress
ISBN 978-1-933868-54-7
Printed in the United States of America

Dedicated to:
Amy,
Misha
&
Zach

House of Glass

Author's Note:

Those of Earth are among the few in the galaxy who are not advanced in the use of thought transfer. The alien Beings on the following pages use mental communication instead of verbal language. This means that instead of quotations you will find this symbol ∞ to show their thought transfers or dialog. It represents the aliens' ability to separate their thoughts into those that are public and those that are private.

Chapter 1

∞

Soluma-Rah stared into the star-filled galaxy from her space ship. She longed to see her home, the planet, TE-Garon, and couldn't wait for the mission to be concluded. Twenty-two transportation discs full of Hu-Mans were all headed back to the snowy zone. But not all of the ships hailed from TE-Garon. There were also ships from Yon-Ya, Fo-Ra and ThAak-Too as well as others.

She, as the Most High Elected of The Federation of Life Sources, felt it necessary to remind all other Beings who traveled with her of their initial Hu-Man pact. Soluma-Rah wasn't sure why, but nervousness tingled through her long appendages as the Most High Beings from seven planets entered the staging area one at a time. Their bodily images floated in a semi-circle in front of her ready for communication.

∞-It is my wish to have collective thought before our ships disperse,-∞ she sent the message.

She wondered if Ka hovered close. He held the position of Most High Being of Celute and was a dangerous enemy. She'd banished him after he initiated an earthquake on the Water Planet. While it resulted in many Hu-Mans evacuating, she'd been unhappy with his decision to act without agreement of the Federation. Did Ka now wait to hear what The Federation of Life Sources would do with their Hu-Mans? She'd forbidden him to take any, yet she seemed to know he'd find a way. He desperately wanted to have some of the Disposables as he called them. Even when she tried to shake it, his angry presence seemed ever close.

11

Soluma-Rah's coral-colored eyes blazed. She remembered how Ka lied to them in the past about removing Hu-Mans from Earth. He'd begun taking them well before the problems on the Water Planet, but what occurred with them was unknown. His planet, Celute, as a whole, had never believed in being kind or peaceful. And Ka had a great tolerance for the internal pain, what was felt in the center of their Being when harm came to another thought projector. More so Soluma-Rah worried he would force the entire Federation into another war with his careless actions.

She shuddered at the memory of those in the Astral Zone lost during the Colossal Fray. Petuk-Rah, Most High Elected from TE-Garon at that time, spent his dying breaths trying to convince her she'd be fine. It broke her spirit to lose her father to such violence, and now Soluma-Rah knew she sought to not disappoint him. Great loss had been felt across the entire Federation during those times, she hoped it would not be so again.

∞-Greetings to all. We are as one,-∞ Most High Bodha from Yon-Ya sent his thoughts and interrupted her memories of the past. He was the last to enter the staging area. While some of the ships were close enough in distance to hear public thought, the staging area allowed those farther away to join in thought communication with The Federation.

∞-Most High Bodha,-∞ she acknowledged.∞-Are your guests faring well?-∞

∞-The Hu-Mans sleep,-∞Bodha thought.

∞-Have any of you felt the presence of Ka?-∞ Soluma-Rah asked the seven members surrounding her.

∞-No thoughts have come from him,-∞ Bodha answered. All others stayed silent.

∞-We must keep our minds searching. We wish no harm to come to his Beings.-∞

12

∞-I worry,-∞ Ora-j, Most High of Fo-Ra, thought, ∞-he started conflict before. He uses fear to gain power over other Beings.-∞

Soluma-Rah sent peaceful thoughts to the Beings gathered before her. She did not want panic to disperse itself.

∞-You are right, Ora-j. And others also hold much power,-∞ Bodha retorted. His head turned to gaze at Rohongra from ThAak-Too.

∞-If two united together, they could be dangerous.-∞ Another's thoughts intruded.

∞-If only Polisis and Duji had never been.-∞ Nods all around met Bodha's thoughts. Duji, the mineral power source kept them alive and in comfort; while Polisis made them beautiful. It created angst among the other Beings that Rohongra controlled power and Ka, beauty.

∞-We must continue to mine for Duji. It will be easier on our Beings with the Hu-Mans helping us-∞ Rohongra quietly responded.

∞-Duji is needed. Our Beings could not survive long without it,-∞ Soluma-Rah agreed.

∞-The need makes us vulnerable,-∞ Bodha stated.

Soluma-Rah's Being became quiet at Bodha's last thought. So true. ∞-That discussion is for another time, for now remember the Hu-man pact.-∞ There were murmured thoughts and then silence as Soluma-Rah began:

∞-Allowable 1: All Most High Beings are in mutual agreement.

Allowable 2: The Water Planet has been evacuated. Each planet shall send representatives who have removed entities for transport.

Allowable 3: As superior Beings, we will be compassionate to those who have been removed.

Allowable 4: The use of these entities will be at the discretion of each Most High Planet.

13

Allowable 5: Those Most High, who wish, may release their transported entities on neighboring uninhabited planets for life sustaining purposes.-∞

Soluma-Rah paused. ∞-Are we still in agreement?-∞ She observed their affirmations.

∞-Have all our Beings recovered from the loss of the Water Planet?-∞ Ora-j's thoughts came through.

While The Federation lived far away in the Snowy Zone, their life sources, sensitive to all creatures in the galaxy, felt the loss of the many Hu-Man lives from the explosion of the volcano and the shaking of the ground that followed across the planet.

∞-My Beings have recovered and are at peace,-∞ Bodha replied.

∞-We are depleted from the journey,-∞ Soluma-Rah thought. ∞-Perhaps we are also anxious to move forward preparing the Hu-Mans for their new life.-∞

∞-There is much to be done,-∞ Ora-j concurred.

∞-Most High, Rohongra, your Being is quiet.-∞ Soluma-Rah pushed thoughts her way. ∞-Has your alliance changed?-∞

∞-My alliance, as always, is to the Beings of ThAak-Too.-∞

Soluma-Rah did not press. Instead she struggled to find the right thoughts to send everyone forward with caution, safety and hope. Her private feelings were jumbled. Soluma-Rah worked to calm her Being before her thoughts became public.

∞-Anxiousness fills us. We have much to learn about the Hu-Mans. Remember to be kind and compassionate as we are all one. Many blessings.-∞

Soluma-Rah received good will before the Beings slowly slipped away. She left her console and quietly fled down the hall. She entered a room to the left, moving her limb so the wall opened before her. Her Being watched the Hu-Mans sleep. Their bodies at rest looked beautiful. Her thoughts returned to Ka. What could he do with such beauty and vulnerability?

14

Soluma-Rah shuddered. She should not think such public thoughts close to the other Beings. In the wrong hands such knowledge could harm the Hu-Mans.

Chapter 2

Before Mandy and her dog, Charlie, entered the Biosphere in Arizona, the Yellowstone super volcano erupted. It created a sonic boom that caused Mandy's ears to ring, and formed a dark cloud in the sky that chased her as she ran to the safety of the Biosphere.

Mandy entered the large building and searched for other survivors, wandering corridors and going up and down staircases. Finally, after not seeing a soul, she stepped into a room, climbed into a bed, and shut her eyes. Exhausted, she needed a moment to rest. She'd been unable to sleep the night before, lying awake obsessing over the fact that her brother Derek, and the cute boy they'd picked up at the gas station, were taken by aliens. Even though Charlie, the American Bulldog she'd rescued, sat close, she hadn't felt safe closing her eyes until she rested inside the dome.

It seemed moments into her restful slumber that a man found her and Charlie nestled on the bed. He woke her and then carefully demanded she follow him, staying well away from the dog, but carrying her two backpacks. Now she stood in the hallway with her fate being decided.

"We can't kick her out," said the plump woman with salt and pepper hair who stood to the left of Mandy. "She's on her own."

Mandy's head hurt and she had trouble concentrating. But she understood. The man didn't think there would be enough food for all of them.

"That one pack is full of food," Mandy interjected pointing. "And I have more in a truck out on the hill."

He scoffed. "We agreed once the other students and workers left here, we would not allow anyone else to come in. It's for all of our protection."

Mandy wanted to speak out again, but didn't know what she could possibly say, especially to the towering and obnoxious gentleman who had found her and stood to her right. She needed the safety of the Biosphere. According to her friend, Gillian, this was the closest and safest place for her to be now. Around the world, earthquakes had devastated cities and The President himself had said humans might not survive. Mandy's fingers found her deceased parents' wedding rings where she'd hung them from her necklace. Tears threatened. Could they really force her outside? Could they let her die?

"I don't care if she's a kid. There will barely be enough for us, let alone a girl and, let's be honest here, a horse. We don't know how long it will be before the government is back in control or how extensive the damage is to the earth. We might have to live in here for years. And that dog, well, she's going to mess with our air."

The woman looked down at Charlie and shook her head. Mandy wasn't sure what that meant. She blinked several times rapidly. What would or could she do?

"We can't let any wanderer in," the man continued. "Start now and we set a bad precedent when others show up."

"You don't even know if there are others," the woman argued. "Listen, I've been a cook and a housemother for years. I'm not going to turn a poor child and her dog out into the volcanic ash. We've plenty of food. Remember, we figured we had enough even if the others stayed."

"Those statistics were all based on guesses. We don't know anything. This situation could be worse than anyone thought. As a physician, I'm educated enough to know we're inviting trouble," the man huffed. "Listen, do you want to risk our lives for a girl and a mutt?"

"Bolton, I'm telling you one more time. I'm not turning this girl or her dog away. Deal with it." The woman turned her back to the man and touched Mandy's shoulder. "Come on, dear. Let's get you cleaned up and settled."

"What if she is one of those aliens?" he yelled from behind them.

Mandy giggled before she caught herself. The skin around the woman's eyes crinkled. "Doctor, you're losing it," the woman said. "The aliens came in peace to take children to safety. They predicted the earthquakes and eruption. They aren't invading or causing harm."

The smile that Mandy wore drifted from her face. Tears tumbled down her cheeks. "They're not all peaceful. And they lied to us. They're taking people by force," she argued. "They took my brother and a friend of ours." She couldn't hold back anymore. Mandy's shoulders shook and her voice cracked.

The woman shot daggers at the doctor before she stepped toward Mandy and put an arm around her. "Oh, honey. I'm so sorry. What happened? Tell me all about it." The woman guided Mandy to a wooden bench set against a white wall.

Mandy started from the beginning. "My family is from Wyoming. I had a friend, who warned me of problems in Yellowstone. She told me we needed to leave quickly. She said to come here. It was the only way we could survive." Mandy's voice caught in her throat. "My parents," she hiccupped, "died. They were badly burned in a fire and passed away a couple of days ago." Mandy closed her eyes. Memories of her parents lying in the makeshift hospital room filled her head. Had it only been a few days? So much had happened.

She felt the woman squeeze her hand. Taking a deep breath, Mandy continued. "My brother and I headed here alone. On the way, we picked up another kid before we crossed the

18

border into Arizona. We thought we'd made it. Then last night, when we stopped, aliens snatched them." Mandy's sobs wracked her small frame. "My brother is all I have. Now he's gone, too."

The woman patted her back. "There. There," she said.

Mandy heard the man's shoes on the tile as they came toward her.

"If . . . I mean when he gets away from them, he'll come here to look for me. I have to stay. At least until then. Please don't make me leave." Mandy turned to the doctor. Her hand reached out to touch his jacket. Her sleeve lifted and a reddened cut was displayed. He quickly backed away. "Please, you have to let me stay," she pleaded, her hand finding the necklace she wore.

"Of course you can stay." The woman stood. She took Mandy's packs from the man. "Anyway, the doctor really doesn't get to say who stays and who goes. It's up to the group." Then the woman took Mandy's hand and led her away. "And I'll put in a good word for you." She winked.

At the far end of the hallway Mandy saw an older man shuffle away. She wiped her eyes with her sleeve. "Thank you," she said. Charlie trailed them both, her tail wagging and hitting the wall as they passed.

"Francine, don't you walk away from me," the doctor called after them. "We're not done discussing this. Lives other than yours are at stake here."

"No more talk, Doctor. We have more pressing problems right now. I'm going to help the others find a way to shut the door properly so ash won't come in. Would you like to help? Or would you prefer to keep screaming at me and possibly have more people enter the habitat?"

Mandy instantly felt a connection to the woman. Francine reminded her of her mother. She took a strand of her shoulder-length brown hair and twirled it around her finger. The smile she shared with Francine forced itself into place hesitantly.

They left the doctor to stand alone in the hall. Mandy hoped the others would be more like Francine and less like the doctor.

Light fell into the walkway, despite the ash on the Plexiglas roof. Mandy fixed her gaze on the ceiling. Suddenly she accidentally stepped on Francine's heel and bumped into her. "Sorry," she mumbled.

They stood at what appeared to be a closed exterior door.

"I guess someone else got to it first," Francine said. "There was a problem with the hydraulics or something, but it's fixed now." She shrugged.

"I did it," the older gentleman said from behind them. "Nice dog," he added. "Welcome."

Mandy hadn't heard him come up behind them. She opened her mouth to reply, but the man shuffled away.

"Come on. You can help me in the kitchen. It's almost time for lunch. After, we'll get you settled in a room," Francine said. "First though we should clean that wound. Normally I'd ask Bolton, but I'm not sure that's a good idea right now. What happened?"

"I ran into a tree branch escaping."

"You poor thing," Francine said. "From the aliens?"

"No not aliens. Well meaning folks had taken me in. But then my brother found me."

Francine pursed her lips. As you probably already guessed, I'm in charge of the kitchen. You'll help me today. Later we'll figure out what you'll do for chores."

"Um. I'm not a good cook." Mandy felt the need to disclose. She hoped it wouldn't cause Francine to rethink letting her stay.

"With the right instruction you can be," Francine told her dismissively.

They walked down a narrow hallway. Framed posters, explaining the history of the Biosphere, covered the walls beside them.

20

"How many people are staying here?" Mandy asked as they entered the dining area.

"Seven including you. Eight if we consider your dog, and we should probably consider him." She patted Charlie's head.

"Her," Mandy said.

"Everyone else left immediately after the quakes and the power outage," Francine said. "They wanted to be with their families in case. . ." Her words drifted off. "The rest of us, we were too far away from those we love. And with the Biosphere being what it is, it seemed like it was safer to stay."

"What is the Biosphere?" Mandy asked while Francine gathered soap and a towel. The friend who had told Mandy about the place hadn't really said much other than she and Derek would be safe there.

"It's a habitat created years ago to see if a group of people could sustain themselves. It's been used for other things since. Most recently they'd-outfitted it to prepare for a Mars expedition. That's good for us. It means the dome should hold against any high winds, the turbines will work even with the ash, and crops will grow and feed us," explained Francine. She rubbed the wound clean then placed a bandage.

"Are you sure?" Mandy asked. She didn't want to cause others harm. "Because I really do have some food." She nodded to the one pack.

"Yes, I am. The Biosphere should be able to house and feed ten. That's according to the specks. At least that what's Phillip says."

"Is that the old guy? The nice one we met in the hall?"

Francine smiled. "Yep. He's been here longer than any of us, which is a very long time. He's kept the dome running for years. We're lucky he stayed. Then there's Doctor Bolton, who you also just met. He's in charge of our health - overseeing oxygen levels in our blood and making sure we don't lose too much weight or have any vitamin deficiencies. I know he seems like a bully. Well, I guess he is a bit. Anyway, Aspen and Evan are, or were, interns. Aspen came to learn animal husbandry from Doctor Pluckett and Evan came to learn more about bugs. Oh, and there's Dagny. She ran the tech center and all the computers. You're going to find her interesting. She's different - quirky - and always has steamy romance novels she's reading, so if you get bored . . ."

They entered the small efficiency kitchen and Francine pulled some celery and broccoli out of the refrigerator.

Mandy laughed nervously. "I don't read-"

"Oh, honey, I'm sorry. But don't worry, I can teach you." Francine stopped and looked Mandy in the face. "My daughter struggled with reading and we worked with her, and now she's about your age. In fact, she's in college." Francine became very quiet. Her gaze drifted off. She blinked rapidly several times and bit her lip. "She's in Pennsylvania. Well away from here. Where it's safe. You'd never know about her reading trouble unless she told you."

Mandy interrupted her thoughts. "Oh no, I can read."

"I see," she said, but Mandy could tell she didn't.

"I just don't read those types of books. Steamy romances."

"Oh." Francine chuckled.

"What y'all laughin' about?" A gorgeous young blond strutted into the kitchen.

Mandy couldn't help but stare mesmerized. The slim girl's eyes glittered an amazing deep, sparkly grey.

"Aspen," Francine said. "This is Mandy. She's joining our crew of misfits. We're talking about reading."

"Oh. What y'all makin' for lunch? It smells delicious."

"Something wonderful. But you'll have to wait and see."

"Ah heard you and the doctor arguing. Everythin' okay?" Aspen asked.

22

Francine nodded as Mandy tried to pull her gaze away from the girl's face. Aspen grabbed a piece of celery off the counter and popped it in her mouth. Mandy's eyes were drawn to a colorful turtle tattoo on her neck.

The girl reached out her hand, palm down for Charlie to sniff. Once "okayed," Aspen pet her. Charlie slobbered happily as she was rewarded with attention.

Mandy stood in awe of Aspen, sure that if the planet hadn't been devastated; the pretty girl wouldn't have ever even spoken to a small town girl like herself.

"Welcome. Hope the doctor's not right about y'all bein' a drain on our food supply or worse yet, an alien." Aspen laughed. "He's such a funny man. He's a hoot, ain't he, Francine?" Aspen didn't wait for a response. "Ah'm goin' to go check on the chickens. See ya in a bit," she said and sauntered away.

"Lunch will be ready in about an hour," Francine said. After Aspen left the kitchen she turned to Mandy. "Don't' mind them. We've plenty of food," she reassured. "And more growing every day. Speaking of food, can you get me some potatoes from the storeroom? It's the door on the left, just inside the dining area."

Mandy nodded. "Come on Charlie, let's go find potatoes." When Mandy opened the door to the storeroom her eyes widened. Shelves piled with food met her gaze. Cans sat tipped over and things had been thrown everywhere and anywhere. Bags and boxes lined the floor and were shoved on top of each other to make more room. Mandy pushed a bag of apples to one side on the shelf and three cans rolled off at her.

"Wow, you okay?" A young guy came up behind her and grabbed one of the rolling cans before it hit the floor. He stared at the ground between his feet.

"Yeah. Yes, I'm fine." Mandy glanced down to see what was there. "I'm Mandy. Francine asked me to find potatoes."

The boy looked up and then quickly away. "Francine sent me to help. Did you find them?"

Mandy smiled. "Are you kidding?" She gestured to the room behind her.

He looked around, shifting from his left to his right foot.

"Yeah, I guess it's kind of messy in here." He leaned over. Muscles rippled under his shirt. He quickly retrieved a bag of potatoes and handed them to her. She guessed this wasn't the first time he'd been in there. "We were in a hurry once we heard about the volcano and all. We took food from all the nearby abandoned homes and, I guess, just threw it all in here."

"It really needs to be organized," she said. He didn't argue. "I'm Mandy."

"Yeah, Francine told me. I'm Evan."

Mandy accidentally touched his hand when she reached for the can he held. He pulled back as if stung. His gaze dashed to the door.

"I'd better get these out to Francine," Mandy said quietly. She shuffled past him.

She entered the kitchen and handed Francine the potatoes. Mandy knew exactly how she could become a valuable member of the team. "I'd like to organize the pantry a bit. Is that okay?" she asked. Mandy picked up her one pack containing food. The other had clothes and a few sentimental items.

"That mess. By all means, have at it." Francine waved a hand and went back to her vegetables.

Mandy's cheeks quickly became flushed as she moved things around on the shelves. She thought of her mom as she worked. Mandy took a deep breath and wished she could smell the sweet cinnamon of the ice cream shop her parents had owned and the lavender perfume her mother always wore. The memory faded and she was back in the storeroom with boxes cluttered around her and perspiration on her brow. She emptied every case and soon all the shelves contained items neatly organized and

24

easy to reach. She stepped back to survey her handiwork. "There. No one will break an arm tripping over a can of beans now," she said to Charlie, who lay with her head between her paws outside the door.

"I can't find anything in the pantry." The voice, Mandy recognized as Doctor Bolton's, filled the dining area. It pierced the quiet of the moment. "I've looked before," he said. "The flax seed oil must be somewhere else."

"I've told you a dozen times. It's to the left on the first shelf. I'm sure if you open your eyes you'd be able to find it on your own," Francine challenged.

Mandy heard the voices coming closer. She cringed and wished she could hide, but saw nowhere to go. Charlie slowly rose, blocking the doorway. Now she couldn't even flee.

"That place is dangerous. The last time I tripped and almost broke my neck. You should do something about that. After all you're in charge of the food, remember?"

"I swear. I told you, it's right there." Francine stepped around Charlie and inside the storeroom. She pointed to a shelf and stopped, stunned by what she saw.

"Francine, I actually moved it here," Mandy said and took the flax seed oil from the third shelf.

"Amazing!" Francine stood in awe and surveyed the room.

"Did you do this?" Doctor Bolton asked. His eyebrows rose.

"It's no big deal. I moved some things around a little."

"A little? It looks great." Francine grinned at the doctor. "All my canned vegetables are together and so is the fruit. No boxes on the floor. Bolton, are you seeing this?" Francine exclaimed.

"I probably wouldn't have put the spices over there, but it's okay," he murmured.

Francine rolled her eyes. "Thanks, Mandy. You're going to be a great help around here. I know it."

Mandy's smile faded as the doctor grumbled under his breath and stomped off. Phillip walked by, a hammer in one hand and a handkerchief in the other. He nodded, smiled his approval and disappeared.

"Ignore Bolton. He's grumpy," Francine explained. "I have to finish lunch. Are you done here? You can help me."

"Okay."

"How about homemade fries?" Francine shuffled toward the kitchen with Mandy a step behind.

Chapter 3

Doctor Thomas Bolton slammed the cupboard door closed. His fists clenched and unclenched. He couldn't believe Francine had argued with him. It only made it worse the girl had actually contributed. Now he'd never get rid of her and the dog. He turned to see Phillip enter the medical center.

"Good. You're here," Bolton said.

Phillip nodded and made his way to the bicycle that sat near the middle of the room. Counters wrapped around two full walls and a door in the back led to a private shower. A patient bed sat in the middle covered with boxes of medical supplies they had found, but had yet to put away.

"Really. You can't get that together quick enough for me." Bolton needed a release. The confines of the Biosphere were already getting to him. Before they'd closed the doors, he'd often run five miles or more on the roads surrounding the facility. He stood with his back to the counter watching as Phillip shuffled across the room.

Phillip knelt beside the bike and arranged the items he'd brought in the day before. Bolton sure hoped he now had everything to put the generator together. Bolton watched the other man's hands work and thought that's what he'd have looked like if he'd been able to get a surgical residency. They weren't that different. Phillip put machinery together, connecting parts that, if cared for, worked as a whole, while Bolton did the same thing for people. Phillip's hands became streaked with grease. Bolton walked over to the sink and quickly used the sanitizer on his own hands. He took a moment to clean the counter while he stood there. What would he do when the sanitizer ran out?

Bolton didn't understand how Francine could be so wrong. The girl and her dog needed to leave. Already their group might be in trouble, what with all the mouths to feed. Not to mention the issue of oxygen and carbon dioxide. And, the worst part, Bolton shivered, dog hair. He picked up the nailbrush next to the sink and scrubbed his fingers vigorously. The idea of dog hair in his food made his stomach roll. He hoped the storage area wasn't contaminated. The other staff, had they stayed, would've supported him. Surely they would've understood. You can't just open the door to anyone. Else they'd all be dead soon.

"You understand my position on the girl, right?" Bolton asked Phillip.

Phillip looked up from the connectors he worked on. He pushed back his cap and scratched his forehead. Bolton thought he would age a day before the man got out a single word. "Yep," Phillip said and went back to his work.

"Then you agree with me? See, if only Francine would listen, we wouldn't be in this fix. We're already worried about oxygen and food."

Phillip raised one eye to the doctor. "I agree with Francine," Phillip said in his quiet timbre.

Bolton reacted as if struck. His hands came up and he waved them in the air. "None of you get it. The entire planet is probably dead or will be soon. It's not our fault we're lucky enough to have a great place to make our stand and perhaps, survive. If we continue to let people in, we'll cut our own chances. Already, who knows if we can make it?"

Phillip kept his head down the entire rant. When Bolton quieted, his head rose. "Just because the planet is dying, doesn't mean we should lose our compassion for others."

"That dog could've brought in diseases. The girl . . ."

28

Phillip rose stiffly from the floor. "It's ready." He stepped back as Bolton strode over.

Bolton climbed onto the bike and slipped his feet into the straps. Phillip plugged the mixer in so it sat on the counter in front of the bicycle. Bolton turned the pedals and waited. "Nothing," he declared watching intently.

"Keep pedaling," Phillip assured.

Bolton grunted and decided whether it worked or not, he needed the outlet for his anger. He pedaled faster. Stupid. Stupid people, he thought as he rode. He didn't notice at first when the mixer turned. "Hey, it works," he said and looked around for Phillip, but Phillip had left the room as silently as he'd entered.

"At least now I can have my algae shake for breakfast," he said to the empty room. Yes, it probably would've made more sense to have the bike in the kitchen for Francine to use, but he didn't care. She could come to him if she needed to mix something. He smiled. He liked the idea of controlling the bike mini-generator.

Chapter 4

∞

∞-Most High.-∞ Bodha of the planet Yon-Ya nodded at the image of Ora-j. ∞-Thank you for agreeing to meet with me privately.-∞ Bodha stood behind the console of his ship where he knew his thought transfers with Ora-j would be protected. They both still traveled the galaxy on their way home with their Hu-Man charges.

Ora-j remained stoic. For a moment Bodha wondered if the thought transfer worked, then he noticed the facial tick. He remained silent and waited.

∞-As peaceful entities we are united in common thought.-∞ Bodha repeated the phrase he'd rehearsed with his second-in-command and good friend, Momur.

∞-Do not speak of common thought. I remain most agitated over the course of events.-∞ Ora-j's figure moved closer to his console, making his projection to Bodha twice as large. Bodha moved back instinctively and winced. Ora-j's image was one that could create fear. While most in the Astral Zone stood smaller in statue, Ora-j's Beings rose almost twice as tall at seven feet. Then too, most of the others either had no hair on their Beings or had it removed, allowing for the Polisis to be more intense in its effect. Not the Beings from Fo-Ra. They proudly wore their coat.

Bodha held back his private thoughts and continued. ∞-I understand your fear.-∞

∞-I think none of The Federation of Life Sources understands.-∞ Ora-j's thoughts gained in intensity. ∞-We made a wrong decision to interfere with the Hu-Mans. Yes, we have

30

felt their loss, but already that loss is removed from our centers. Mark me; they will lead us to battle.-∞

Bodha had not envisioned the transfer would go this way. He sucked breath in and then, when he could hold it no longer, expelled the tension from his body. He repeated this process until he noticed Ora-j's breath equaled his own. It was a technique that the Beings of Yon-Ya had perfected called Ten-Dati. ∞-Whatever our individual thoughts, we are one in the Council and must support Soluma-Rah. If not, none will surely survive another war.-∞ Bodha saw Ora-j relax. Ten-Dati, the use of breath, had the ability to calm all but the most intense of Beings. Those of Yon-Ya had used it during the Colossal Fray to survive when others in the Zone had given their life force in protest against the Beings of Celute.

∞-Hu-Mans will cause much pain,-∞ Ora-j finally transferred.

∞-Not if we can control the ones we carry in our holds.-∞

Ora-j's eyes narrowed. ∞-We would not have proposed to evacuate the Hu-Mans, but since we have them, we have agreed to use them as workers.-∞

Bodha felt disgust. Quickly he hid his private thoughts once more. ∞-Each can do as they wish. Soluma-Rah made that clear. My Beings, living in such close proximity to the planets of Celute and ThAak-Too, are fearful. We know both Ka and Rohongra plan to use the entities for mining purposes. They refer to them as Disposables. What does that say to you? They will quickly use and discard the beings Rohongra carries. And with Ka having none – well, he shall surely be on the prowl to acquire his own. When they need or want more, where will they turn? They will come to Yon-Ya. They will cause harm.-∞ Bodha could guess at Ora-j's private thoughts at that moment. Ora-j was most likely incredibly glad to live on a planet at the other end of the Astral Zone.

∞-Why did you wish to transfer thought with me?-∞ Ora-j inquired.

∞-As I've always been clear, we will not bring Hu-Mans to the planet Yon-Ya. I know there is a rock that orbits your star where they can survive. I wish to gain your approval to let them go on Wadding.-∞ Bodha thought.

∞-What! You make a claim that Ka and Rohongra are dangerous allies now, and then you wish to place what they want most on the rock of our home? Never! We are supremely pleased our star system is as far from your – no, our enemies. I cannot willingly allow you to endanger our Beings. Take them to another system.-∞

∞-Our ships are not as stable as yours. We would never make it to another system and back. Also, we have no knowledge of other zones. We could travel for ektons and never find a suitable home. What if I place them on the rock farthest from your star? What if I leave them on Terrat?-∞

∞-They would still be in our system. It would be a risk to the Beings of our planet.-∞

∞-No one will know. Only Momur, my second-in-command, and myself. I can keep the location from all others.-∞

Ora-j rubbed his face with his limbs. ∞-Terrat?-∞ He nodded. ∞-I only agree because we are in common thought about the Hu-Mans. But do not make me regret my acquiescence.-∞

∞-Never, my good friend. Never.-∞

∞-When do you wish to transfer them to the rock?-∞

∞-We shall follow you now.-∞

Ora-j nodded and disappeared.

"That went well," Momur said.

Bodha released breath. "It did. I'm not sure if it occurred because my arguments about Ka and Rohongra dominated, or the thought that if he and his people wish to use more of the Hu-Mans they will be close and the only ones who will know they are there."

32

"You cannot control Polisis."

Bodha thought on the phrase. They used 'You cannot control Polisis' to refer to all that could not be. "As a young Being I believed otherwise," Bodha said.

Polisis, the most valuable of all minerals shone brightly on the bodies of those who had much. They used it to adorn themselves. The most powerful had garments, while the lesser Beings would make rings to adorn their heads, necks and limbs. Only those on Yon-Ya refrained from wearing the mineral. That did not mean they didn't appreciate it. Instead, they used it to create beautiful forms in the sacred places. It seemed so unfair of all their planets, all Polisis could be found only on Celute. Bodha had often dreamed of having the ability to take the ships of Yon-Ya and search the Astral Zone for the valuable mineral. Yet, now that he had become thought leader, he'd become as impotent as all others before him. Even if they had explored and found Duji, the power source used by all in The Federation, it would have enabled Yon-Ya to be a force. But instead his Beings had Ten-Dati and the power of calm.

Bodha placed a limb on his friend and their thoughts became one. ∞-We must not think of the Hu-Mans and their new home once we've left them.-∞

∞-Even without thought, we will be at great risk. Ka will hunt you down. Hunt me down.-∞

Bodha's limb traced the outline of a muscle on Momur's face. ∞-We cannot hide. Our skin and our life force prevent it. Ka would find us no matter where we are. It is best we stay with those of our own.-∞ Momur was more of a warrior than all others. They embraced. ∞-Clear your thoughts and set the course.-∞

Momur nodded. ∞-And you?-∞

∞-I shall retire and ponder how to control Polisis.-∞ His lip curled.

Chapter 5

Dagny leaned back in the office chair situated in the tech center, flipped off her sandals and crossed her ankles on the desk.

"Ah don't know what to do," Aspen Langley paced in front of her. When she turned, Dagny smiled at the jade-green turtle tattoo that seemed to crawl up Aspen's neck below her hair. "Ah mean, what was ah thinking? Ah don't know anythin' about animals. That's why ah came here in the first place. What my internship should've taught me," the young woman ranted.

Dagny saw no reason to interrupt Aspen's tirade. Instead, she sucked on a cherry lollipop and fingered the novel she hoped to finish once Aspen left. She knew she should feel guilty about reading while everyone else made sure all components of the Biosphere were in order and working. But as the computer tech, could she help it if the computer bank in front of her had no reason to be powered on? Suddenly aware the room was silent, she looked up.

"Well?" Aspen demanded, her hands on her hips.

Dagny shrugged. She had no idea of the specific question. "Well what? You want me to say, 'Go home? Quit?'" She smirked.

No one would leave. Not anymore. Probably not even if they wanted to. Her glance moved across the room. She imagined the white paneled Plexi-glassed dome above the agricultural area. The "grow lights" were all that would keep the plants alive. Already ash had blotted out the sun and covered major portions of the roof.

"Ah can't do it. Ah've chickens, goats, pigs and sheep and, and I know nothin' of any of them. Not really. Ah mean, ah've only been here for what? A few weeks."

"Yeah, about the same amount of time as Evan, and you don't hear him complaining about having to care for all the plants." Dagny plucked a hair from her shirt and let it drop to the floor. "And he came to study bugs."

"So what are you sayin'?"

"I'm saying, get over it. Think of it as real world experience," Dagny said.

"Sure, and what if the animals die? Then what of our real world experience?" Aspen lifted her arms and shook her head. She quickly dropped her hands to the desk and leaned over, her face much closer to Dagny's. "You don't get it. Ah don't know what to do. And your dang computers are down. Ah need the Internet. Ah need to figure out why the chickens aren't eatin'. And ah need to do it soon or we won't be gettin' any eggs."

The corners of Dagny's mouth lifted. "Wouldn't make a difference if the computers booted up right now, because the Internet is probably still down." The power along with the Internet had crashed as soon as the aliens left the atmosphere, just as they'd said it would. And while she wondered if there were people who had survived, none of them knew how many there might be and where they could hide. They'd heard about the alien evacuations and the damage caused by the numerous earthquakes around the world. Of course that all occurred before Yellowstone erupted. Dagny shook her head; she doubted things would ever be the same.

When the first earthquake hit, she had a brief moment where she thought about leaving the Biosphere, but it disappeared in a second. Where would she go? She had no one left. An only child of divorced parents, her mother had been killed by cancer and her father by alcohol abuse. An aunt lived somewhere in Louisiana, but she hadn't seen her in twelve years.

Since then, all her friends had been found on the Internet. People she'd never even met other than in a chat room. So without any other option, Dagny stayed.

Shock registered on Aspen's face. "How can the Internet be down? Ah mean really, what's goin' on?"

Dagny sighed. "The world as we knew it no longer exists, sweetheart. In fact, this could be bad, really bad. Plenty of books have been written about what would happen to the Earth if a super volcano, like the one in Yellowstone erupted. None of the scenarios were promising. Really, this might be how it is for the rest of your life, however long that might be. Cooped up under a dome with a few animals, a bunch of plants to eat and a group of crazy people. Crazy because you'd have to be to believe we can make it through this." Dagny dropped her feet to the floor, stood, and stretched.

Still Aspen made no move.

Dagny shook her head and sat again. Boldly she picked up her book and opened it to where she'd left off. What more could she say to get Aspen to leave?

"Why didn't you go with the aliens?" Aspen asked, her brow furrowed and her voice small.

Dagny thought before speaking. She chewed her upper lip. "I was the borderline age," she finally said. "Truthfully, I didn't know if they'd take me and it seemed like a lot of effort to be turned away. Staying here seemed easier." As the plump girl all through high school and college, Dagny had been overlooked enough. She didn't think she could've handled it if the aliens hadn't picked her, either. "I don't know." Aspen's gaze held her mesmerized. She studied the young woman's face and remembered the night before when she'd dreamed of Aspen with facial tattoos. She thought how Aspen, with her short almost silver hair, looked a bit like a warrior princess.

"Ah couldn't go," Aspen finally admitted.

"Sure you could've. Bolton is mean, but he let the others go. He didn't even question them about staying. Not even Pluckett." Pluckett who'd been the farm manager and who would've known why the chickens weren't eating.

"Bolton doesn't really want anyone else here, but he needs someone to order around. Ah can't believe he thinks he gets to decide who stays and who goes."

Dagny blinked. She hadn't been there to hear the fight, but Aspen had been quick to fill her in. Still, she hadn't really come to a conclusion about the girl and her dog staying. She looked again toward the dome and shook her head. Making the girl leave would most likely be a death sentence for the kid.

"No, ah couldn't go," Aspen repeated and looked away. "Sugar was in labor, about to lamb. Ah couldn't leave her with no one to assist, in case, in case . . ."

"Lambs? One of the sheep had lambs?" Dagny's face lit up. Her grandmother had always made the best lamb chops with cherry sauce. She thought back and tried to remember if any of the stuff they'd taken from the neighbor's pantries had cherries on the label. She licked her lips. "Hot diggity," she said. Ever since the others left and she'd heard they'd be on food rations, and might even have to eat seaweed, Dagny couldn't stop thinking about food. It wasn't the first time. She always felt this way when she went on a diet of any sort, and dieting had been her way of life. Diet, binge, diet, binge.

"Yes, ma'am, Sugar had two lambs. They're so sweet." A smile played across Aspen's face and replaced the fear that had been there since she'd entered the tech center. "You should come down and see them."

Dagny shook her head. She had a rule against seeing food on the foot. "Do you remember seeing any canned fruit in the pantry? Never mind I'm sure there's some."

"Can't you think of anything else but food?" Aspen asked, and then as if sensing the reason, her face became flushed. "Oh, my. No!"

Dagny refused to admit her thoughts and prove Aspen correct, so she changed the subject. "Listen, you know more than you think. Those little chicks will be fine in no time."

Appeased briefly, Aspen pulled on her dangly earring. "Ah hope so," she said.

Chapter 6

Evan sat at the table in the dining room, one of the seven that now met for dinner. He watched as Charlie's eyes followed Mandy as she walked in with a plate of burgers. Francine followed with a steamy plate of fries.

"I hear you, Charlie," Evan said as he licked his lips. The smell made his mouth water.

"I can't eat this," Doc spat out at Francine. "You know I don't eat meat." He pushed himself away from the table. His lip curled and he wrinkled his nose.

"No worries Bolton." Francine shuffled back to the kitchen, returning seconds later with a plate of vegetables and a small amount of nuts on the side, no dressing. She placed it gently in front of him. "There you go," she said.

"Oh," he moved the carrots around his plate as the others passed food.

Evan carefully took his burger, hoping there'd be leftovers. He knew this would probably be one of the last times they'd get to enjoy this kind of meal. Which set him wondering, once they ran out, if he'd ever eat beef again, period. Or even see a cow. Cows hadn't made the list of animals kept in the Biosphere.

"Listen everyone. I have an important issue to discuss," Doc announced loudly.

Evan turned to see Mandy feed Charlie half her burger and some fries. Charlie gulped down her food, licking her chops and waiting expectantly for more.

"Now that we have extras staying here with us, it's important we're closely monitoring everyone's oxygen levels and weight."

Evan wondered if this meant Mandy and her dog were safe. He'd heard from Francine what Doc had said about it and knew her feelings.

"After dinner I need everyone to see me so we can establish current weight levels," Doc said as he stared at Charlie. "Evan, where are we with the plants?"

Evan quickly chewed a mouthful of beef. He swallowed and stuttered, "The plants?"

"Yes, now that everything is closed up, are we losing oxygen in the soil?

"I haven't seen any wilting or anything unusual." Evan's breathing increased. Doc had a way of making him feel inferior.

Doc nodded. "Well, please keep me updated."

Evan watched as Phillip, who sat on the other side of Mandy, placed his hand below the table and held out some of his burger waiting for Charlie to take it from him. Doc glared his way, but Evan didn't think Phillip noticed or, if he did, cared.

"Sir, ah also have somethin' we need to discuss," Aspen sang out.

Evan's palms began to sweat as he heard her voice. He looked up from his plate glancing at her. He felt his cheeks warm as their eyes met and he looked back down at his burger. The uncomfortable silence caused beads of sweat to line his forehead.

"There's a problem with the chickens. They're listless and droopy. You - we need them and ah haven't been able to bring up any information on the Internet."

Evan wished he could feel more comfortable around Aspen. She was the first girl he'd found himself really attracted to. And he had an opportunity now to really get to know her – after all they were both stuck here. Why couldn't he get his anxiety under control? He wiped his hands on his pants.

40

"Chickens can eat anything we do. Maybe you need to feed them something different?" Francine said.

"Yes," Dagny agreed. "Maybe, we should feed them the tasteless burgers we're being forced to call dinner."

"I did my best with what we have. We have to be smart and careful," Francine said. "Which means saving spices and salt right now."

"Aspen, do the chickens have grit?" Mandy quietly spoke.

"What's that?" Doc asked.

"It helps the chickens break down the food they eat," Aspen explained. "Yes, they have grit."

"Do you think they're bored, hungry or maybe they need more water?" Mandy inquired.

"Chickens get bored? I've never heard of such a crazy thing," Doc said.

"A friend of mine back home raised chickens and she used to give them orange peels to play with. Chickens can't eat them, but it entertains them."

"Well, isn't that interesting," Francine said. She directed a look at Doc.

Aspen nodded. "Ah wondered if they are getting enough hydration. What do ah do if they's not drinking enough water?" she asked.

"You put water in a smaller bowl and put their beaks in it. Or if you have a dropper you can give it to them that way," Mandy said.

Doc rose from the table and cleared his area. The rest of the group followed suit.

Evan lingered, hoping to be near Aspen for a second longer. He was rewarded when she walked over to Mandy and whispered. "What do ah do if they're not eating?"

Mandy turned, dropping her voice barely above a whisper too. "You could bring them in your room and hand-feed them."

"Why would ah bring them in my room?" Aspen stepped back.

"According to my friend, sometimes after a disruption they have a hard time bouncing back. Like when a coyote gets too close. When this happened she'd bring the chickens inside and hand-feed them every couple of hours. Eventually they calmed down and could be returned outside."

"Are you nuts? Ah can't have a bunch of chickens in my room!"

"Well, maybe you could try for a little while. Of course, you'd have to wake up every few hours to feed them."

Mandy picked up her plate and walked into the kitchen. Aspen shook her head, and followed with Evan close behind breathing in her scent. Thinking about Aspen had become the only reason he didn't get emotional at meals. Staying in the Biosphere had not been an easy decision for him. Somewhere out there he had brothers, a father and a grandmother, only he didn't know where. Those who remained at the sphere had agreed they would not discuss family once the doors closed. At the time it had seemed like a good idea. While he kept quiet during the day, his nights were filled with dreams.

Evan put his dishes in the sink and waited to see if he was needed. Francine waved him off and he left. In the agricultural area, plenty always needed to be done. This helped him from focusing too much on what he'd lost.

Chapter 7

Mandy woke and stretched. Silence greeted her. For three days now she could hear rain on the roof in certain parts of the Biosphere. In the living quarters however, nothing was heard but the animals in the bay below. Charlie snored lightly next to her. The sage green blanket had been kicked off by both of them during the night and now lay in a heap at the bottom of the bed. Mandy moved a little closer to the middle, trying not to disturb Charlie. Every night, she would start off in the center of her twin mattress, while Charlie lay on the edge curled up. However, it never failed, by morning Mandy hugged the side and Charlie commandeered the majority of their bed. She thought about making Charlie sleep on the floor, but that seemed cruel.

She stretched again and sat, looking at her reflection in the large round mirror across from her bed. Her hair stood out around her face. Ugh, she sighed, "I need a hair-cut, Charlie."

Charlie snored, ignoring her. Maybe Francine would help. Lately she hadn't been spending a lot of time in the kitchen. Instead she tried to stay busy helping where needed. She'd spent one whole day organizing and rearranging the two-story private quarters Phillip had given her to use, but mostly she worked in the agricultural area.

She climbed out of bed, no reason to delay the inevitable. Her stomach started to growl. Charlie stirred next to her. They'd established a normal routine of sorts. They rose around the same time every day. Mandy would take Charlie down to the animal pens where her dog helped with creating fertilizer, they ate breakfast with Francine, cleaned up, and then went to work. After morning chores, Mandy spent time staring out the blocked window, searching for mountains that were out there, but she couldn't see because of the falling ash. She'd also read some of the leftover agriculture journals in the bookcase in her living area. Around lunchtime, she would join Francine, eat, clean up and then spend some time holed up in the rainforest talking to the mysterious animals that crawled about until dinner.

Mandy had quickly become close to the easy-to-talk-to Francine. Dagny, Doc and Phillip never seemed around except for meals. Aspen and Evan could be found, but they both appeared overwhelmed with the immensity of their responsibility and generally had books they studied.

Reaching into her dresser, Mandy pulled out clothes for the day. An easy pick. She had only what had been in the one backpack the day of the explosion. At some point, she thought she would be able to get to the truck she'd driven to the Biosphere to get her other suitcase, but she knew now that would be impossible. She probably wouldn't be able to find the truck, even if she tried. Mandy sighed again. She'd gained a couple of castoffs from Aspen, but Mandy didn't have the courage to wear the brightly colored shirts and cut-off shorts yet. She lifted a shirt from the drawer. It was her brother's. Somehow when she'd packed, it had become mixed with her things. She lifted it to her face and sniffed, but it no longer held his scent. Mandy quickly dressed, and then wound down the spiral staircase to her private living area, absently touching the wedding rings of her parents she wore around her neck. Charlie leapt out of bed and trotted right behind her.

Mandy had rearranged the furniture in her living space, but had second thoughts about how the desk sat against a window that no longer held promises of a view. Mandy felt homesick. She missed her parents and brother so much. She blinked quickly and rubbed the moisture from her eyes. Every time those thoughts occurred she tried to tell herself she should

44

think of it like she'd gone to college, only with a dog as her roommate. Sometimes it helped the feelings of despair that threatened to overwhelm her. Sometimes it made no difference at all.

She was lucky she had Charlie to keep her company because it sure had its perks. Charlie kept her on her toes. While the others didn't have anybody to talk to, Mandy did. She understood the rule about not talking about family, but Mandy found it almost impossible. Every thought she had was attached to her mother, father or Derek. Every uncomfortable silence seemed filled with tears she refused to shed in front of the others. She wanted no one to have a reason for her to leave.

Mandy pulled back the odd peach curtains, left over from some previous occupant. They covered a large bay window that opened to the hallway. Dagny walked by, her nose stuck in a romance novel, completely oblivious to Mandy and her curtains.

"Let's go, girl."

When Mandy entered the animal bay, the place instantly filled with the sound of sheep, lambs, goats, chickens and pigs. She called out to Aspen, but received no answer. She wandered around greeting the animals while Charlie did her business.

"You hungry, girl?" Mandy scratched behind Charlie's ears the way she liked. "Come on. Let's go eat. Now remember girl, you have to be good. Today, you have to leave people's shoes alone. No chewing on them. They are not food." Charlie stared at her and barked. "Okay, come on." Two days prior, Mandy had been in the medical center getting her vitals taken and her arm checked, when she looked behind Doc and there, crouched low, sat Charlie chewing on the back of one of Doc's expensive leather loafers. Mandy choked and gave Charlie a stern look. She didn't want to make Doc any angrier about her presence than he already was. Charlie chewed a moment longer and then, becoming bored with the shoe, rose to sniff around.

Mandy and Charlie left the animals and followed the path to the stairs. She climbed with the dog a step behind until they entered the black and white-checkered dining area. Francine stood where she always did, in the kitchen.

"Good Morning," Mandy said.

Francine smiled. "Oh, hello dear. I didn't hear you. You and Charlie ready to eat?"

"Yep," Mandy grabbed a bowl and filled it with oatmeal from the stove. "Have you seen Aspen? I wanted to see how the chickens were doing?"

"She's already eaten and left dear. How'd you sleep last night?"

"Good. You?"

"Oh, fine, just fine." Francine seemed preoccupied.

Mandy wanted to ask what she thought about but didn't think it would help. Mandy knew she worried over a daughter in Pennsylvania. Out of the corner of her eye, Mandy saw Phillip. She turned, ran across the room, and hollered his name. But as usual, he'd already disappeared behind another door down the corridor.

"Phillip is hard to track down," Mandy stated.

"Yes, he's been very busy."

Mandy finished eating, rinsed her bowl off in the sink using recycled water, and went to try and put it away when Francine took it from her. "Go on. Scoot!" She shooed her out of the kitchen. Mandy reached to pick Charlie's bowl up off the floor, but it was gone too. Mandy looked at Charlie to see if she had pieces of the bowl in her mouth, Charlie cocked her head to one side.

"I'm just checking," Mandy said. "I think you've eaten worse before." Mandy turned. "Francine, are you sure you don't need any help?"

"I've got it, dear."

"Okay, then see you later." Mandy and Charlie headed away from the living quarters, and to a staircase that led to the agriculture biome. Below them lay an expansive farmland being used to plant potatoes, a vegetable garden and another area for any other item that could be harvested for food. Mandy knew they were currently trying to grow rice. She entered the animal bay.

Aspen huddled in the middle of the pens on her hands and knees. Mandy's eyes opened wider. She'd never pictured Aspen as the type of girl to get her hands dirty.

"What you doing, Aspen?"

"Lookin' over some manure. Accordin' to the log book, ah need to analyze how the pigs are eatin'. You okay?"

"Charlie and I came to see if you needed any help with the chickens?"

"No. They seem to be doin' better. And ah'm about done here."

"Aspen, please. What can I do to help?"

"Well, ah guess the pens need cleaned. Ah'm kind of tired. Ah've spent the last few days tryin' to work with the chickens, gettin' them to eat. Ah even had Evan check soil levels to make sure its not givin' off too much $Co2$, and causin' problems with the air."

Mandy grabbed a bucket and quickly started putting manure from the sheep pen in it. "Aspen? Do you like living here?" Mandy knew the question sounded dumb.

"Well, yeah. It's better than the alternative, isn't it?" Her brows rose.

Mandy nodded. "I know we've agreed to keep family thoughts private, but I really miss my brother and friends. I lived in a small town my whole life. Went to kindergarten and all the way through grade school with the same eight kids. Of course, in many ways, living in the state of Wyoming is like living in small town. You know everyone; it's not six degrees of separation more like one. I belonged to the speech and debate team and we'd travel all over. We'd get to know all the kids our age. Meets between different towns felt more like family reunions. In fact, we were competing the day the first earthquake hit."

"What happened?"

"Everyone scattered. I guess some stayed in Wyoming. One girl's parents took her. Once we knew there was a problem with Yellowstone, my brother and I decided to flee and meet up with a friend in Alaska."

"Alaska?"

"My friend had family there we could stay with. Another friend, whose parents are scientists, said it would be far enough away from the initial blast to survive." Mandy blinked several times.

"How'd you end up here?" Aspen asked.

"It was our second choice. Honestly, we ran out of time so we went south instead."

Aspen looked off away through the doorway, as if making sure they wouldn't be disturbed. "Ah miss certain things, too. People." She shook her head. "But it's important we stay focused on what we have here. In the mornin', ah like to sit on the beach and listen to the sound of the waves. It reminds me of a trip ah took with my parents to Mexico. And when ah'm feelin' lonely, ah go down into the warmth of the Savannah. The savannah reminds me of home."

Evan rounded the corner and the girls fell silent. Aspen walked to the pig's pen while Mandy finished loading up the last bucket. She smelled disgusting.

"Hello," Evan squeaked, wrinkling his nose.

"Hi," Mandy said.

"Um." Evan cleared his throat. "Aspen do you . . . do you have the manure ready for me?" He stared at his feet.

"Yep, right over there." She pointed at where Mandy stood without looking up. She seemed oblivious to the awkwardness of the situation.

Evan quickly looked at the bucket in Mandy's hand. "Oh. Thanks I'll take that." He reached for it brushing against Mandy's knuckle. Evan flinched and Mandy set the bucket on the floor.

Evan grabbed it, put his head down and walked away mumbling good-bye. Mandy stared after him, wondering if he would ever feel comfortable.

"You have anything else for me to do?"

"Ah should have had you check with Evan," Aspen said absently, her focus on the watering system. "He has much more under his control. Why don't you head out and see if he needs you to weed?"

"Sure," Mandy said and quickly slipped out. She saw Evan heading away and followed.

In her room the day before she had found the special notes of a female scientist who'd stayed in the Biosphere during the first experiment. She'd read how it had taken weeks for the garden to be fully operational. Mandy now had a better understanding of how much it would take to make this work long term. She wondered if Evan would be able to speak to her long enough for her to figure out what needed to be done in the agricultural center.

Chapter 8

∞

∞-Are the Hu-Mans at rest?-∞ Dahi, the thought leader of ThAak-Too invaded her mind. He reclined on soft pillows, his Being overflowing even the spacious confines. He'd adorned himself with much Polisis, as he wished for his Being to be noticed.

As a member of The Federation of Life Sources, they had participated in the evacuation of the Water Planet's youth. All Hu-Mans under the age of twenty-four, who had wanted a chance at life, now resided in the holding areas of The Federation's transportation disks. The rest had been left behind.

Rohongra stood before him, weak. Not long after they left the Water Planet's atmosphere, the planet turned on its own and many became energy once more. The process of losing life force in the galaxy drained Rohongra. She intensely felt each soul rise and join with the universe.

∞-The Hu-Mans are at peace,-∞ she finally thought.

They pumped a mixture of gas and oxygen into the holding area to allow the Hu-Mans to quiet for the long voyage to ThAak-Too.

∞-What of our other transportation disks? Have they reported in?-∞

Rohongra, as Most High, knew she should be the one in power, and asking the questions, but she had little doubt within her who really controlled their planet.

Dahi disgusted her, not because of his largeness, but because of his desire for Polisis and consequently Duji, the mineral their planet mined and sold to the other Beings of The

50

Federation. For this energy, they received Polisis. While Dahi used the shiny material for enhancement, those who mined needed it to make sheaths to protect their bodies from the poisonous effects of Duji. To Rohongra it was a futile endeavor. Mine a mineral to purchase protection that allowed you to mine for a mineral. Yet, she knew Duji provided energy for the rest of The Federation too. Even so, she believed there had to be another way.

Now they transported Hu-Mans with the intent to use them in the mines. No one knew how long these new beings would survive the harshness of their planet's star.

∞-I have authorized the council of ThAak-Too to establish a settlement. We shall land at Goul and remove the Hu-Mans.-∞

Rohongra felt too weary to object to Dahi's overstepping.

∞-Then we shall analyze the Hu-Mans. Some of them are useless to us now. We will have to wait while we manipulate their growth, but eventually, they will be of service.-∞

Rohongra nodded. Only those Hu-Mans who stood less than four feet tall could enter the mines. Hu-Mans taller would be used for above ground mineral extraction. Those too young to work would have to mature. And Dahi wanted them all now. She wondered if he had collaborated with Ka to determine exactly how to manipulate the Hu-Man's growth. She shuddered to imagine what pain the effort might cause the beings that slept below in the hold. What pain it would cause her, and the others, who lived in synchronicity.

∞-You may leave now. I have much to consider,-∞ he thought.

She was dismissed. Dahi had become more and more of a problem. Rohongra's violet eyes narrowed as her mouth formed a line. ∞-I will leave you,-∞ she offered. Her garment covered the length of her body and made a slight rustle as she moved her Being.

Before she could even turn, she felt the pain. ∞-Ahhhhh!-∞ she screamed confused. Her right limb fluttered to her chest. She touched the area where her Being connected with others of life force. Immediately the pain increased. She fell to the ground. Her breath became shallow. How could it be? Dahi? What of Dahi? He seemed unmoved although his head tilted to one side. She searched to see his thoughts. They were closed from her.

When she finally had gained enough strength, she rose. Her entire Being shook.

∞-We are no more,-∞ she said simply.

Dahi remained silent a moment before he answered. ∞-I believe our world is no more. They are no more.-∞

* * *

∞-According to the Code of The Federation, it is considered an inexcusable act to enter another planet's atmosphere without a ruling from that planet's Most High Council. I have not been able to transfer thought with Most High Bodha or the Beings from his planet to acquire this ruling. ThAak-Toon's vessels, therefore, will be asked to remain outside Yon-Ya's atmosphere.-∞ Soluma-Rah stood tall at her console, an almost incredible task considering the situation. The transportation discs would soon enter the Snowy Zone - almost home, she privately thought.

∞-You ask the impossible!-∞ Rohongra rebuked. The pain of her planet's death had paled her normally blue skin to almost white. She knew this made her violet eyes shimmer more than normal. She had no idea what had happened, only that her planet's life force and those of its Beings had been silenced. Rohongra needed help and it seemed those of Yon-Ya were withholding it, or perhaps it was Soluma-Rah. ∞-What is your reason? Those of Yon-Ya are peaceful Beings. You state The Federation's purpose is to unite us all. Yet, you would be willing for more ThAak-Toons to perish for the Code. You do not give the truth to me.-∞ Rohongra's thoughts waivered. They needed to land on Yon-Ya and empty their holds of Hu-Mans so they could journey the remaining distance quickly and hopefully arrive in time to find survivors.

Dahi stood outside the screen's view. And with him so close, she dare not appear weak. She shared a glance with him. Dahi's skin appeared to not suffer, nor was his heart-shaped face wrinkled from pain. She wondered how he withstood the anguish she swam in. What could have happened to their planet?

∞-We have increased our speed to full capacity. At half-light we should enter our own atmosphere and be available to transport the Hu-Mans from our holds to our planet,-∞ Soluma-Rah thought. ∞-Once that is complete, I will arrange to meet your transportation discs and transfer your Hu-mans to our holds. Until that time, you must await us.-∞

Dahi shook his head. His eyes drew together and his neck enlarged.

∞-If you compel us to delay, we will have no other option but to eject the Hu-Mans into the Astral Zone. We cannot wait.-∞ Rohongra didn't want to appear to beg, but the pain in her center increased.

∞-You have agreed to be compassionate to the Hu-Mans. And if you land on Yon-Ya, it will be deemed you are committing an offense against the Code,-∞ Soluma-Rah warned.

∞-The Hu-Mans should not be wasted. Relay the message, we will be landing in peace, but make no mistake – we are landing on Yon-Ya.-∞ With that last thought Rohongra shuddered and withdrew her thoughts, closing the connection between ships.

∞-You have appeared in distress,-∞ Dahi reprimanded. ∞-As leader it is un-thinkable to be seen as such.-∞

Rohongra grasped for strength enough to rise above him. ∞-Do not think you have the ability to judge me. Remember whom our Beings take guidance from. Now leave me. You will not join with those who land on Yon-Ya. Instead, you shall lead the first ship to ThAak-Too. You will evacuate those who are still alive on our planet. It is only fitting, as you are part of the reason we are now being punished. Your greed has created this. You are the one who encouraged us to go deeper into the planet's center. To take all. Now with no heart, the planet is finished. Our home will be no more. We are forced to become outcasts. And who knows how many survived.-∞

Dahi lifted one side of his mouth. ∞-You are right. You are the one they look to. The one they will blame for this. And I, as the one who has tried to give you council, will be the one they will now look to for guidance. Once we relocate, I am sure you will no longer be Most High. And what of the others in the Federation? I'm surprised they have not already figured out that they have lost their access to energy. They seem more concerned with the Hu-Mans than with the fact their planets can not survive long on what they have stored.-∞

Rohongra had thought about what the loss of energy would mean, but she would give Dahi no inkling of her private considerations. ∞-We in the Astral Zone lived before Duji and we shall survive after as well.-∞

Dahi leaned forward, his extreme body jiggled and resettled with the effort. ∞-Yes, we lived without Duji in the past, but those Beings who did are no more. Those who have life force now have never had to live without. They know nothing of the challenges. They are weak. You are weak. Dump the Hu-Mans and perhaps we can still find remnants of the planet to harvest energy from.-∞

∞-Dahi, I am planning on a mission to rescue our Beings, and instead you would argue that we should attempt to harvest energy. Your thoughts are impure.-∞

54

∞-My thoughts are what will keep us in power.-∞ Dahi spat.

He left and Rohongra sank to the floor, her breathing, labored and painful.

Chapter 9

The following day Mandy left Aspen at the animal pens to search for Phillip. She'd found him elusive. She took the winding path past the plastic-covered door of the rainforest, into the scorching desert biome and finally down to the dry air of the savannah. She hadn't ventured around the Biosphere much, staying in the agricultural area, the animal bay or upstairs in the lodging area. Aspen had told Mandy the cement walkways had been replaced to help with CO_2 leakage. Plastic covered the area to her left, which helped protect the ocean and rainforest from each other. Most of the information Mandy had read about the Biosphere confused her. The scientist's notes left in her room had talked in scientific formulas and ratios.

Her feet made a weird thudding sound on the footpath. It sounded loud against the quiet of the biome around her. The only thing, which could be heard in a few places, was the whirring of machines in the basement.

Once in the savannah, Mandy realized she'd forgotten to ask Aspen about animals that might lurk in the tall grass. The temperature change and humidity caused her hair to stick to her forehead and the grasses tickled her legs. It gave her the willies. She shuddered, took a deep breath, and waded through. Charlie whined at her heels.

Mandy headed toward the unused fan in the far corner of the room. When she reached that area, Aspen said she should see a metal airplane-looking door on the right. Mandy smiled, thankful for Aspen's directions. She had avoided this area and would've been very lost without them.

Quickly she reached the entrance to the basement, realizing the walk hadn't been as bad as she'd imagined. She grabbed hold of the handle and tugged. Her hand slipped and she landed in the dirt. Charlie sat, her mouth open and tongue flapping.

"Are you laughing at me?" Mandy asked, as she wiped herself off. She reached for the door a second time, firmly planted her feet, and pulled as hard as she could. The door opened to a dimly lit tunnel, a whoosh of air chilled her instantly. She didn't know if she would ever get used to the temperature changes inside her new world. They regulated each of the biomes for its particular survival. All of them created their own tempos, which together made a perfect harmony, according to Aspen.

Mandy thought the rounded tunnel held the promise of more secrets. A small stream of water ran in a culvert between her legs. She could see beads of condensation forming on the ceiling. She walked with her feet on the side of the structure, not wanting to get them wet. Mandy thought it looked like a slip-n-slide, only at the end she would thud into a hard, metal door instead of landing in the middle of a backyard. She reached the end of the tunnel, and firmly grasped the handle of the door. Luckily, this one opened much easier.

She stepped into a large, dark-gray, circular room with a strange rubbery roof. A bright red fire hydrant sat in the middle, with a pool of water surrounding it. Charlie barked when she saw a figure across the room. Mandy covered her ears, while Charlie whined and sank to the ground.

Phillip held a finger to his lips as he walked toward Mandy and Charlie. Charlie crawled close to him, her tongue hanging out.

"No treats, girl," he said quietly, petting Charlie. "Need something?"

"What is this place?"

"We call it the lung. The metal walls cause acoustic issues. The water helps, but you still need to be quiet."

Mandy noticed Phillip wore a gray janitorial coverall and heavy work boots. It seemed strange as she normally saw him in jean overalls and black t-shirts. Mandy looked behind him. Thick plastic covered what looked to be a door. Another piece lay on the floor. Phillip shifted to his left, blocking her view.

"Whatcha need?" he asked again.

"I wanted to say thank you for the room."

"No problem."

"This is a really cool place. What's it for?"

"It's how the Biosphere breathes. Too much pressure and the dome would pop. The ceiling is neoprene. It allows the roof to move up and down with pressure changes."

Mandy liked the quiet man and knew he could teach her a lot if she could spend time with him. She wished he didn't like being alone so much. She nodded to the area behind him. "Why is there water in here?"

"It's from irrigation. The original designers thought this room could be used in case of a fire. This hole fills up with water from condensation and can be replenished."

Mandy had never heard Phillip talk so much before.

"So we don't get electricity from here?"

"No. There are generators in the basement under the Agriculture Biome."

"Generators?" Mandy's voice rose an octave. "Don't generators take gas? Wouldn't we need a lot to keep this place going?" Mandy nervously rambled.

"Not gas-powered generators."

"Oh." Mandy wiped the sweat from her forehead. Not gas, then it had to be sun. That made sense. "Sun-powered?" But the sun now lurked behind clouds of ash. "But then, we'd be in serious trouble," she added.

58

"Not sun. We have turbines. The scientists here hoped they could use wind technology for the future colonization of Mars. Great for us. Most of the wind-powered turbines are extremely touchy. These have been made to withstand almost any conditions."

Mandy nodded absently, thinking of her good friend, Gillian, whose parents had been geologists. They had planned to go and live on Mars. That was how Gillian knew about the Biosphere. How she knew it would keep Mandy safe.

"Okay, you'd better run." Phillip turned his back and headed for the plastic-covered door. Mandy and Charlie followed a few steps behind. Mandy wasn't ready to leave yet. Curiosity consumed her.

Phillip sighed when he turned and saw her. He finished tying his boots and asked, "Can you hand me the spade?" He stood and reached for a jacket on the hook next to the door. He put it on.

"What are you doing?"

Phillip picked up a gas mask. "I'm going to shovel ash away from the door. Rain and ash mixed together hardens like cement. This door is slightly protected from the elements. Later we might need a way out."

"What's the plastic for?" She pointed toward the door.

"I don't want ash to blow back in. That's why you and Charlie should leave."

"Is that safe? You going out there?"

Phillip ignored her. "I also noticed a fire along the hill. I want to make sure it's not coming our way." He placed a gas mask on and then put the jacket hood over, pulling the strings tight. Next, he put on work gloves and grabbed the spade from her. Charlie began to growl in the back of her throat.

Mandy stumbled away from him and across the room. She watched Phillip as he pulled the plastic back. Bumping into the door, she grabbed the handle and wasted no time yanking it open. She tripped, but managed to catch herself before she slammed her face on the floor of the tunnel.

The door closed behind her. Panic filled her lungs. What if contaminated air filled the dome? The door closed and shut her in the cold, dimly lit tunnel. With Charlie at her heels, Mandy focused on putting one foot in front of the other until she reached the safety of the other door. Back in the savannah she took deep breaths, dry air filled her lungs.

* * *

Bolton stepped onto the white sand of the beach. In front of him the ocean lapped at his feet, while behind him palms towered. He'd come down from the medical center for a coconut. He climbed the palm and retrieved one, dropping it carefully to the sand. Now he stood over it confused. The ocean. He could see tiny fish swimming but . . . something didn't feel right. His brows drew together. Finally he realized the pumps were not working. "Oh, no!"

He left the coconut where it had landed and hurried down the path toward the savannah. The first group who inhabited the Biosphere had a problem with the ocean. Bolton remembered their algae scrubbers had stopped working. He couldn't remember all the details, but knew the carbon cycle could be affected if the pH of the ocean changed. How important, he didn't know. He had to find Phillip right away.

He was almost jogging by the time he reached the savannah. He hopped back and fell on his butt as one of the numerous garter snakes slithered across the path. Quickly he jumped to his feet and brushed himself off. His hands shook. He searched the grasses with his eyes, wary now of other snakes. He knew they served a purpose; otherwise he might have lobbied for their demise. Carefully he took a step forward. "Now I'm coming through," he said to anything listening. "Just you stay away. Do

60

you hear me?" He could see the top of the door through the weeds. He stopped.

"I'm sorry. Were you talking to us?" Mandy asked, her hand on Charlie's collar.

Irritated, Bolton ignored her question. "What are you doing?" he demanded.

"I went down to the lung to talk to Phillip."

"Great, I'm looking for him. We have a problem." Bolton pushed past her.

"He's ah," she mumbled and then called after him. "Doc!"

He ignored her blabbering and slammed the door between them.

When he'd originally arrived to accept the position in the medical center they told him he had to take a tour. Immediately he remembered why he hadn't been to the lung since then. He carefully walked down the concrete tube, mindful to keep his hands away from the disgusting walls and his feet out of the stream of water. Jubilant, he finally spotted the door at the end of the tunnel. "Phillip," he called as he entered the lung. Then remembering the acoustics, he quieted. He stepped out onto the landing and looked around. The lights in the lung glowed dimly and made it difficult to see across the room. "Phillip?" he whispered.

Receiving no answer, Bolton descended and stepped into the large, round room. He shivered. Darn. Now where could Phillip be? He had a habit of being where he shouldn't when you didn't need him, but now that he was needed, he'd disappeared.

Bolton knew another entrance existed. In fact, there were two. One that went outside and another that led, well he couldn't remember for sure but somewhere in the basement. He drew closer to the wall so he could find a door and that's when he saw a faint shimmer. Curious, he crossed the room. A large plastic tarp lay on the floor in front of a plastic covered doorway.

Bolton got his bearings. He thought he stood at the outer doorway.

His gaze, drawn to a set of work boots he recognized as Phillip's, then found a pair of overalls that hung beside the door. Before he could move a muscle, the door swung out and a man stepped close to the plastic with a weapon in his hands.

"Phillip?" the doctor shouted and then covered his ears as he once again remembered the acoustics.

The man behind the plastic shook himself and then emerged. The weapon appeared to be a spade that was set to one side before the man walked toward the plastic mat. Bolton jumped away. The man wore a gas mask and hooded jacket. Bolton felt reasonably sure Phillip stood before him and his anger rose.

He watched as the man stepped onto the plastic tarp and then proceeded to pull off his jacket. Particles sifted in the air as ash dropped from creases when the man moved. He waved an arm at Bolton, but Bolton had already moved back from the dust.

"You went outside," Bolton hissed as he leaned towards the man. "No one is allowed outside. How dare you risk our safety?"

Once he removed the jacket, Phillip untied and stepped out of heavy work boots. He still had not removed the gas mask. He waved Bolton back again. Then he unzipped his coveralls and dropped them to the floor until he stood in front of Bolton in his boxers.

"I want an answer," Bolton demanded.

Calmly the man stepped off the mat. He moved to one end and folded the tarp to the center. Then he moved to the other side and folded that in as well. He continued until the tarp completely covered the clothing and boots. Only then did the man remove his mask.

"You should've left. You know the ash is dangerous if it gets into your lungs," Phillip whispered.

"Exactly. What were you doing out there? Who said you could go out?"

Phillip removed his overalls from where they hung and slipped his feet into his other boots.

"Did you need something, Bolton?" he asked.

"Something is wrong with the ocean, a pump, or maybe the algae scrubbers. I don't know. Something. But it's not as important as figuring out why you went outside and what you did."

"Okay. I'll check the ocean," Phillip said. He ambled toward the door Bolton had known existed but couldn't find.

"Wait. I want an answer." The fact Bolton had to whisper only made his anger worse. He ran to catch up to Phillip who already headed out the door. "You can't just do whatever you want. No one here can without affecting the rest of us," Bolton's voice rose. "This is why there has to be someone in charge." He spoke to Phillip's back all the way to the pump room.

Phillip never turned to respond. Instead, at the pump he knelt and went to work.

"This conversation isn't over." Bolton turned to leave. His lips pursed and his eyes narrowed. "How do I get upstairs?" he asked through clenched teeth.

Phillip pointed. Bolton thought he caught a hint of a smile, but in the dim light he couldn't be sure.

No worries, though. He knew he'd certainly have the last laugh.

Chapter 10

∞

∞-You should not have advanced?-∞ Soluma-Rah projected her thoughts directly to Rohongra. ∞-We still have not received permission from Most High Bodha.-∞

Soluma-Rah knew Rohongra had entered Yon-Ya atmosphere and now prepared to land.

Soluma-Rah was only partially angered by the ones from ThAak-Too. Deep inside her own Being, she knew she carried at least partial blame. She had thought and felt the problems of ThAak-Too, but chose to ignore the plight of the Beings; really they were also her Beings as part of The Federation. Most High Ora-j from Fo-Ra entered the transmission space and Soluma-Rah quickly acknowledged him. Soluma-Rah felt great pain from Rohongra and it took her a moment to regain her focus.

∞-All of you knew. You feel. Have felt. You chose your own gain.-∞ Rohongra's thoughts rang painfully true. There were murmurings from the five other Beings in The Council. Rohongra looked away from her screen. Her Being had seemed reduced under the stress of losing so many ThAak-Toons.

Soluma-Rah's thoughts turned to what would happen when her own planet's power reserves were depleted.

∞-We informed you we would land and our need to remove the Hu-Mans from our holds. They slow us on our journey.-∞

∞-I am sorry. It will be considered an act of war if you do. I cannot allow the Beings of Yon-Ya to be subjected to that kind of stress.-∞

∞-We have no other choice.-∞

Soluma-Rah felt the increasing pain of Rohongra's desperation. Where had Bodha disappeared to? Why had he not thought? After the Colossal Fray, The Federation made a pact to let no neighbor enter another's planet's outer edge.

∞-You want to release Hu-Mans?-∞ Soluma-Rah asked.

∞-That is all. So I can quickly help the Beings on my planet.- ∞ Rohongra covered her center with her limb. ∞-Delay means more loss of life force. You will send more ThAak-Toons to our death?-∞

∞-What about Ka? You are almost as close to his planet.-∞ Ora-j asked as he twirled a Polisis ring around his shortest appendage.

∞-We have no time.-∞

Soluma-Rah felt the pain in her chest increase. She had no answer that would stop the suffering. Soluma-Rah closed her mind for a moment to gather her thoughts.

∞-I fear there is no other solution at this time. I recommend we allow the ThAak-Toons to unload the Hu-Mans. I will continue to attempt to contact Most High Bodha.-∞ Soluma-Rah moved away from the console.

* * *

∞-We should never have gone to the outer edge of the Snowy Zone. This is the consequence of our trying to control that which is not ours to understand.-∞ Momur's body swirled in agitation. ∞-Now what should we do?-∞ According to Ora-j's latest thought transfer, ThAak-Toons would soon enter their planet's atmosphere. ∞-They shall see we've not prepared for the Hu-Mans. They will know our innermost thoughts. Hu-Mans will no longer be safe anywhere in the Astral Zone. ThAak-Toon's anger may be turned on our Beings. And what if it is just a ploy to take our Duji reserves? What if that is their true reason for landing?-∞

Bodha felt the truth of his friend's words. He'd informed his planet of the necessity to help the Hu-Man's, but had left out any details of what that would entail. All along he'd planned to relocate them to the other end of their star system. He hoped the Hu-Mans could learn to survive on their own. Located on the opposite side of their galaxy, Terrat seemed too small for most to even give it a passing thought. For the Hu-Man offspring, it seemed perfect. But taking the Hu-Man's to Terrat would only save them if no one knew their whereabouts. ∞-Rohongra is more moderate a leader. She will express no anger at our choice. In fact, it was spoken of at council. What may anger her though, is our desire to keep the Hu-Man's final location secret. As for the stores of Duji, they are safe from thought.-∞

The communal door opened with a hiss. Both Momur and Bodha made private their thoughts as one of their Beings entered the room. ∞-Most High,-∞ the Being bowed low, ∞-we have received thought ThAak-Toons are nearing Yon-Ya. Their planet is destroyed. Rohongra, through Soluma-Rah, has asked the council for permission to land on our planet. The council is dismayed and unease is spreading to all our Beings. We should return at once. We should turn our ships and go home.-∞

∞-Most High Bodha is not called to action by their thoughts.- ∞ Momur chastised.

∞-But what of our Beings? We cannot leave them to the ThAak-Toons.-∞

Bodha rose and hovered over the lesser Being. ∞-You will do as instructed and continue on our present course. Now go.-∞

The door hissed closed. Momur swirled faster. ∞-You must ask the ThAak-Toons to honor the Code of The Federation and not land. They must wait for us to arrive. We can then assist by moving the Hu-Man's to the planet ourselves.-∞

Bodha nodded. He placed a limb on his friend's head to stop his dreaded movement. ∞-You are right. Open the thought

66

transfer, but be careful we cannot allow Rohongra to know of our location. We shall ask her to wait till our return. We must remove the Hu-Mans to Terrat first. It is unfortunate we shall not have time to assist the Hu-Mans in getting settled, but it cannot be helped. Are we aligned?-∞

∞-It is as you wish.-∞ Momur swept out of the room.

Bodha pondered that which was now truth. As Supreme Leader of Yon-Ya, he alone knew of the location where their energy was stored. If Rohongra, or more likely Ka, were to attempt to take that which they had, it would mean the ending of his life force. Still he had to think of the future. What would his Beings do without Duji? How could such intelligent Beings be so reliant on one energy source? They knew Thak-Too was in trouble and yet they had not thought to find an answer. Bodha, even, regretted the additional use of Duji to power the ships to Terrat. He had put his Beings in danger, all to protect other life forms.

Momur too quickly returned. ∞-There is no more thought communication between others and us. This ship is old. Our devices used.-∞

∞-Then we must hurry to fulfill our duty,-∞ Bodha thought. After all, he was a Being of his word and thought.

Chapter 11

Dagny sat at the kitchen table, her feet crossed and draped across one corner. With the falling ash the external light source had dimmed. Dagny found the kitchen was the one area where the lights were always on and a bit brighter. She had a historical romance in her hands. The cover art depicted a dashingly handsome pirate leaning over a swooning maiden. Dagny bit her lower lip as she read. The romance heated up.

She jumped when Francine accidentally slammed a cupboard door closed. "Sorry," she said.

Dagny didn't even bother to answer. The pirate had leaned closer to the maiden about to . . .. Dagny absentmindedly picked up a sausage left over on her plate from her breakfast. As she put the link to her mouth, she became aware of someone coming.

Doctor Hottie rushed into the dining area. His eyes found her and quickly moved on. Dagny dropped the sausage to the plate and pulled her feet off the table.

"Did you know Phillip went outside?" he demanded of Francine. He stood with his hands on his hips and his back to Dagny. She smiled. Nice jeans, she thought.

"What? What's going on?" Francine wiped down the counter, never meeting his eyes.

"I caught him coming in. He went outside."

Francine stopped her ministrations and stared at him. Dagny carefully marked her place in her book. She stood, straightened her shirt, and ran a hand through her hair before joining them at the counter.

68

"I can't believe he'd do that. There must have been a good reason. Right?" Francine looked at Dagny.

Dagny shrugged and stepped closer to Bolton so their arms touched. He, just as quickly, stepped away. At the intercom, Bolton shouted for Aspen and Evan to join them.

"Wait a minute. Calm down," Francine said. "You're going to scare everyone out of their wits. Phillip wouldn't do anything to jeopardize us."

"Do you know what it means? Him going outside?" Bolton asked.

Dagny didn't, but she was interested in hearing. "What?"

Francine ignored her. "You're overreacting. Are you sure he even stepped outside?"

"What does it mean?" Dagny tried again.

"I'm trained to observe people. Of course, I'm sure. I saw him walk in covered with ash." Bolton looked around the room. "It's probably in the air already."

Dagny squinted trying to find the particles.

Evan ran, coming in from the agricultural area, out of breath, Aspen right behind him.

"What's wrong?" Aspen asked.

Bolton's face reddened and perspiration lined his upper lip. Dagny found it delightfully appealing.

"Phillip went outside. I caught him." Bolton smirked. "This is why I keep saying we need to put someone in charge. We need a leader. Someone who will look out for all of us."

"And of course, who do you think that should be?" Francine demanded, her hands on her hips. "You?"

"I'm certainly the most intelligent one here," Bolton threw back. "Listen, we can't have people going around doing their own thing. It puts the rest of us in danger. Don't you see?"

"Is there a problem?" Mandy asked entering the room.

The group looked at her and Charlie, then quickly returned to their conversation.

"Y'all, has anyone talked to Phillip and asked him about it?" Aspen's hands flew through the air. The room went silent. "Y'all said you saw him. Didn't you ask?"

"He wouldn't tell me what he'd done," Bolton admitted. "But no matter what, we should've known he was leaving the Biosphere and had a discussion about it. You can't leave whenever you feel like it."

"Ah'm not comfortable talkin' about this when y'all don't know why he went out there. So where is he now?"

"He's working on the ocean," Bolton said.

"What's wrong with the ocean?" Francine asked.

Dagny moved to Bolton's side, giving Evan and Aspen room to move closer. She saw Mandy cross to the kitchen table and sit. She wondered fleetingly if the dog would eat her sausage, but then Doctor Hottie spoke.

"The pump is broken."

"Does this have anything to do with Phillip going outside?" Evan stepped forward and asked.

"All of you stop right now. The issue is we need someone in charge. A leader. Someone who can make sure these types of things don't happen." Bolton's voice rose as he spoke each word slowly.

"You're the most impossible man. I can understand why Phillip wouldn't speak to you." Francine stepped away from the counter. "I wouldn't answer you either if that's how you spoke to me."

"Where do you think you're going?" Bolton yelled to her retreating back.

"I think I'll go find Phillip. I can ask him what's going on," Francine turned to answer.

Dagny didn't see Phillip enter, but heard Francine's gasp when she ran into him.

"Excuse me," Phillip said.

70

Bolton, in the middle of the room, approached quickly. Dagny saw him clench his fists at his sides. He was so buff.

"Great! Now we're all here, we can settle this once and for all," Bolton said.

No one else spoke. Phillip's gaze found each one of them. He looked down at Francine, then back to everyone else. "I need some help," he said, "with the ocean."

* * *

Mandy stood on the beach in a used wet suit with a snorkel mask on. She breathed in and out slowly through a plastic tube. She'd never swam in an ocean before, in fact, she'd never even seen an ocean. Freaked out a bit about the idea of sharks in the water, she was pleased they all knew what inhabited the dark, deep pool that was the Biosphere's ocean. Phillip stood next to her telling her about the wave boxes. "You need to check them first. Maybe something is stuck inside." Mandy tried to focus on what Phillip said, but the loss of circulation in her left foot from the fin made it hard to concentrate.

"Mandy, Mandy, are you listening? You have to leave the tube above the water no matter what. Otherwise you will suck in a bunch of water. Take a deep breath before you go below the surface. When you get under the water, there should be three boxes. See if something is lodged in one of them."

Mandy nodded. She took a tentative step toward the water and tripped in her fins.

Phillip steadied her. "It's easier if you walk in backwards."

She did as he instructed. It was still awkward, but so much better. She put her face in the water. She took in a deep breath then slowly let it out. She walked out further and looked towards Phillip and Charlie who stood on the beach. Charlie panted and paced. Mandy gave a thumbs-up and continued until she couldn't touch the bottom.

She took another breath, put her face in the water and floated. A striped fish looked at her through the mask before it quickly darted away. Mandy turned to watch it leave. Water filled her snorkel and she came above the surface sputtering. A commotion on the beach caused her to turn.

Charlie splashed as she ran straight at Mandy..

She spit out the snorkel. "Charlie! Stay!" Mandy shouted.

Charlie paddled, and quickly reached Mandy. The dog nudged her. Mandy kicked hard to pull Charlie through the water and back to the beach.

"It might be best if she waited outside," Phillip suggested.

Mandy, took off her fins, grabbed Charlie's collar and led her down the beach and out the side door. "It's all right girl, I'll be back to get you."

Charlie shook water from her fur and whined.

"Dumb dog," Doc growled. Mandy, so focused on Charlie, hadn't realized Doc stood beside them. She looked into cold eyes. Water dripped from his chin.

"Oh, sorry. I didn't, I didn't…" Mandy stammered.

"Never mind," Doc stepped back.

"Charlie stay." Mandy shut the door, turned, and went back to the ocean. She put on her fins and, this time, didn't hesitate to enter the water. With the snorkel in place, she entered the aquamarine pool. Mandy swam on the surface and practiced breathing while she searched for the fish she'd seen earlier. After a minute, Mandy gave up and headed toward the back of the ocean area where the pipes were. She held her breath and dove. As Phillip expected, no water came out or went into the wave machine. She popped above the surface and signaled Phillip.

She dove deeper, reached her arm out and hoped she wouldn't touch anything slimy. Phillip informed her the boxes turned water constantly to make the ocean's waves. The box turned, sucked in water, then turned again and let it out. Three identical boxes sat next to each other. Phillip had explained the waves were important for the ocean. Without water movement the algae wouldn't be able to grab food.

As soon as Mandy descended, she saw box two was stuck. Mandy reached her hand in. She felt something round and hard. She swam deeper to get a better angle on the problem. She wrapped her fingers around the object the best she could and pulled, but the object didn't budge. Her fingers, when they slipped off, touched the slimy side of the wall. Mandy recoiled.

She twisted her body to one side, to gain better leverage. She reached both hands in this time. Now she could move the object side-to-side. One hard pull and it dislodged. Mandy immediately felt the ocean water begin to move around her, she kicked to the surface.

Phillip stood on the beach next to Evan. She swam to them and handed Phillip the object. He stared at it.

"It's a coconut," Mandy broke the uncomfortable silence.

Phillip nodded and headed away from the beach.

"So, you fixed it. Nice job," Evan said.

Mandy nodded. "Where's Doc?"

"Francine told him off. He stormed out."

A smile spread across Mandy's face.

"What's funny?"

"Charlie, wet, shook herself all over him. It must have been right after he left the meeting."

Evan chuckled. His dimples showed. "Why did Phillip ask you?"

"Ask me what?" she said.

He nodded toward the water. "Why did you get volunteered to go into the ocean? I wouldn't expect a Wyoming girl would know how to dive."

"Oh, I don't. Phillip asked me because I fit in the wetsuit. Apparently the only one left here that he could find belonged to a smaller woman who maintained the ocean. He said if I didn't wear it, the cold water would prevent me from getting anything done. Phillip talked me through how to breathe and dive with the snorkel. It was sort of fun. It's really different down there. You ever been in an ocean like that?"

"No. Lucky for Phillip you could swim."

"Did y'all fix it?" Aspen asked as she walked toward them.

"Yeah," Evan answered for her.

"Oh, cool," Aspen said. "Evan, ah've got more fertilizer for you. It's kinda piling up, if you know what I mean. Do you want it now?"

Evan nodded and followed Aspen out, leaving Mandy staring after them. She took off the fins and headed away from the beach to find Charlie. Her thoughts went to her brother, Derek. She wished he could've been there to see her. He'd wanted her to come out of her shell. Now everyday she learned something new and it made her proud. The terrible things that had happened only made her stronger.

Mandy let Charlie out and stooped beside her, hugging the dog tightly to her chest. "One day I'm going to find him," she told her best friend. "And Derek will be so pleased." A smile spread across her lips. A small black butterfly floated by and landed on her shoulder.

Chapter 12

Evan sat at the dining table and cleaned his eyeglasses. He did it purposefully so he didn't have to enter the conversation surrounding him. While he understood someone needed to be in charge, he didn't really care whom.

He thought about his family. He had no idea where his father was. He'd departed for Africa a few weeks before the eruption. As a mountain climber, he often led groups around the world. While most of the time Evan could get him on a cell phone, sometimes that wouldn't be the case.

Frustration had filled him after the first earthquake. Evan closed his eyes and fought to keep tears from them. His mother had been one of the many casualties in South Dakota from the massive earthquake that started the whole Yellowstone thing. Evan put his glasses on. The rule preventing them from talking about family had been put in place, he thought, because of him. After the first earthquake when the aliens restored power, he'd called and spoken to his grandmother. That's when he first learned what had happened back home. He had been a mess with his father gone and his mother dead. He couldn't function. His brothers were still out there somewhere. He'd wished they and his grandmother had come to Arizona, but she refused to consider leaving the farm. If he'd had a vehicle, he'd have gone to them. He rubbed his eyes. No matter what argument he'd given her, she'd remained steadfast. Now he wondered if any of them still lived. His hands became fists that lay in his lap. Without any conscious thought, his face turned toward the windows. Covered with ash, they effectively sealed the lot of them from the outside. He turned back, his shoulders curled inward. Really, though, did any of them stand a chance?

Evan looked up when Francine slammed his bowl of chili on the table. He'd been at the Biosphere for more than six months and he'd never seen her so angry. Of course, he and the other interns had kept out of her way. Doc didn't get it. Evan considered Francine someone you didn't want to cross.

"Can't we have our meal and not talk about this for a few minutes?" Francine asked.

"Frankly, no. We need to get this settled and right now. I've been saying we needed to choose someone to be in charge from the moment we six first decided to stay in the Biosphere. And no one listened. Now we have people coming and going as they please. Doing who knows what with the limited supplies we have." Doc's voice rose as he waved his arms around in the air.

They did have limited supplies of certain things, but the Biosphere had been created to allow for self-sufficiency. Lots of closets and cubbyholes were filled with stuff. Phillip seemed to know what they all contained, but Doc had wanted it inventoried right away. Evan knew it hadn't been done yet, and wondered if he'd get stuck doing it if Doc became their leader.

Evan's gaze scanned the table. Aspen sat across from him, her eyes fixed firmly on her dinner. Mandy also seemed to ignore the fight that circled them. Only Dagny clung to every word.

"Where's Phillip?" Aspen asked.

Doc scowled. "For all I know he might be outside again. Which is exactly why we need to have this conversation."

"I think he's still working on the pump," Mandy offered, which caused the doctor's frown to turn to her.

"Sit down and eat," Francine told Doc. "Or I'll give your meal to someone who'll appreciate it."

Doc sat and picked up his spoon, but Evan noticed he made no move to eat.

76

"I don't want to be difficult. But I feel very strongly about this."

There was no question in Evan's mind Doc spoke the truth. His gaze shifted to Francine. She sat at the head of the table. Evan's lips lifted slightly. He wondered if Doc recognized the meaning of where she'd positioned herself. Francine reminded Evan of his best friend's mother. She always worked to make sure everyone felt cared for, something his own mother had not excelled at. But also, Francine was a take-charge sort of person.

They really hadn't had much contact with each other before the earthquake. The Biosphere had throngs of people who worked and resided there. Each of them had their own area they were learning, teaching or monitoring. Only after the earthquake, when they learned of the aliens, had they come to really know each other. Most everyone fled the sphere immediately, leaving to join family. Those who remained stayed because they really had no other choice. They had nowhere else to go or no way to get there, or, as in the case of Doc, no desire to go.

"Listen, y'all, if havin' a leader means ah can eat in peace, ah'm all for it," Aspen spoke up.

Evan gazed at her, wishing she would for once really see him. He felt so alone in the Biosphere, in the world. She caught him looking and quickly he ducked his head. If only he didn't feel so nervous around girls.

"Please pass the salt," Mandy almost whispered in his ear.

He knew why she tried not to be noticed. Doc hadn't said anything for days now, but everyone knew he wasn't thrilled about the dog or Mandy. She had to be worried. If he became their leader he could easily force her to leave if he found a good reason.

"Really, do we need to put someone in charge?" Francine's elbows rested on the table.

"Sure we do," Dagny said. She smiled at Doc.

"For everyone's safety," Doc added.

Evan didn't know what to think about Dagny. He hadn't had much interaction with her even after they were locked in. Her bossy manner and wild red hair frightened him. A wizard on the computer, she had assumed he too, would be interested in computer technology mainly because of his age. Unfortunately, Evan had spent most of his young years, hiking, and camping with his father, out where no computers or gaming components could be found. Dagny had an opinion on everything. Her opinion of Evan seemed to be low. Once again, he hadn't measured up to what others wanted from him. He rubbed his neck. Some of her other opinions made him nervous.

"Okay, then. Let's take a vote," Aspen said. "Ah vote for Francine."

Evan watched as Doc's face turned maroon.

"I think Bolton should be in charge," Dagny quickly said. "After all, he has the most education."

"Oh, who cares about education? We need someone we all like and can trust. That's Francine." Aspen focused her gaze on Evan. "So that leaves it up to y'all," she said.

All eyes turned to him. Evan choked. "What? What about Mandy? Who do you think should be in charge?" He turned toward her.

Before Mandy could say a word, Doc informed the table, "As a trespasser, she really has no say."

Mandy bit her lower lip.

"Of course, she has a say," Francine argued. "She's here to stay. She's in this with us."

"Evan, come on. You know who the best choice is," Doc spoke firmly. "Remember where you come from?"

Evan blinked. He knew Doc referred to the fact his mother had been a physician. But that hadn't made her any smarter than his dad. It only made her elusive and distant. He swallowed.

"I vote for Francine." Phillip had entered so quietly Evan hadn't noticed.

Doc stood. "Your vote shouldn't count either," he said.

"Why is that?" Francine asked.

"I think that is apparent. We're having this discussion because of him," Doc said.

"That doesn't mean y'all, he doesn't get to cast a vote," Aspen rose to her feet as well.

"Evan?"

Evan shrugged and looked at Francine.

Doc pushed back his chair, knocking it to the floor, and stormed out.

"Thank you. Phillip, are you ready to eat?" Francine asked. She went to the kitchen and dished up a bowl.

Evan watched as Dagny shoveled the last of her food into her mouth. "I'll go and check to make sure Bolton is okay. After all, he's a very important member of our group," she said.

Mandy waited until Dagny left the room before she spoke. "So I guess Francine, you're in charge now. Does that mean Charlie and I can stay?"

Francine grinned.

* * *

Dagny had attempted to follow Bolton from the dining hall. She wandered by his room and the medical center. Both were locked and most likely empty. Frustrated and with nothing to do, Dagny made her way to the technology center.

All of the computers lay dark. She shook her head. She'd never before felt so lonely. Of course, she thought, she could go back to the dining room, but she knew they'd all be celebrating

Francine's win over Bolton. She could also read, but she felt too agitated to sit still.

Dagny turned to make sure no one saw, then carefully lifted the back from one of the computers. She reached in and grabbed a handful of miniature dark chocolate candies. Quickly, she returned the computer to its natural state. She sat and one by one savored her treat.

She'd never been without online friends before. Normally, she had spent eight hours a day visiting with other techno geeks. The queen of social media, how would she ever survive now?

Even the chocolate didn't console her. Tears filled her eyes and rolled down her cheeks. This was so unlike her normal upbeat and positive self. How did people do it hundreds of years ago? How could they live without communication? Of course, they'd had radios back then.

Dagny dried her eyes and sat up straight. "They'd had radios," she told the room. Her eyes scanned the banks of computers. "Two-way radios."

Not that long ago, she'd laughed with a friend online about how his father still used a two-way radio to communicate. But the government used them too. Dagny jumped to her feet and waddled over to the large storage compartment. Vaguely, she remembered when she'd first come to the Biosphere. She'd been shown, by the previous tech geek she'd replaced, some old equipment that had filled a cabinet. Maybe? Wiring and cords splashed out when she opened the doors. Her mouth pursed. Her eyes searched and her hands dug deeper.

A radio. That's what she'd seen. A two-way radio stuck way in the back. When she finally reached the box, she carefully placed it gently on the counter. Dagny had no idea when it was made, but based on the appearance she guessed a long, long time ago. She flipped on the switch, not surprised when it immediately didn't start up. Seeing no plug, she figured it required a battery.

She picked it up with both hands and walked back to the kitchen. She noticed both Mandy and Francine were slaving over the dishes.

"I'm looking for Phillip. Do you know where he went?"

"He said something about going to the rainforest storage," Francine said. "What do you have there?"

"I think it's a two-way radio."

"Radio?" Francine hurried over.

"I found it in a cabinet. Do you think there might be others out there who've survived?"

"I'm sure there are survivors. Oh, Dagny!" Francine gave her a hug. "Maybe we can talk to them."

"I'll get Phillip," Mandy offered, already running out of the room.

Dagny grinned. Oh the possibilities!

Chapter 13

∞

Yon-Yas surrounded Rohongra's transportation disk. She had instructed that as many of the Hu-Man's as possible be squeezed into the hold and now she waited to step out onto Yon-Ya for the first time. Her father had often traveled the Astral Zone, but that was before The Federation, and the ending of the wars between them. To her knowledge this would be the first time since the Code a Most High Being had stepped on another's planet.

∞-Are you sure it should be you?-∞ A thought came to her from one of the many around her waiting to remove the Hu-Mans.

∞-It can only be me.-∞ She drew together what little strength she had left. She needed to hurry and unload.

She had sent Dahi to ThAak-Too. Now she waited to hear how many had survived. Her color returned and she knew this meant one of two things; either the death was over because the planet had stabilized or more horribly, those ThAak-Toons no longer existed. She feared what Dahi would find.

A ramp descended. She had made the decision to approach those of Yon-Ya without her protective Polisis armor. She hoped her display of vulnerability would ease the fears of Bodha's people.

She nodded to those waiting to open the doors. Once opened, she floated down the ramp.

∞-Most High Rohongra.-∞ A bald, oval-faced Yon-Ya approached her.

Rohongra bowed in deference to the Being in front of her. She knew she didn't have to, but with the deaths of so many filling her inner Being, she did so without regret.

∞-We have come in peace to unload the Hu-Man evacuees.-∞

The Yon-Ya nodded and lifted a limb to signal her to rise. ∞-We have felt the pain of your planet. All our thoughts are one with you. But we know naught of what you do. What we know is you are in violation of the Code of The Federation.-∞

∞-Surely Most High Bodha or Soluma-Rah has informed you of our desire? We wish to unload the Hu-Mans and leave to evacuate our planet immediately.-∞

∞-We have heard nothing of our Most High since he left the Astral Zone with you and the others of The Federation. I shall confer with our council. You must wait for our answer.-∞

Rohongra watched the Yon-Yas as they left her presence. Soon she grew frantic. The Beings had departed and seemed to not be in a hurry to return. She knew nothing of their culture, their way of doing. Worry filled her. She'd be too late to save her people if she did not act quickly. She turned to the ramp of her transportation disc. The Hu-Mans waited to be released. One young Water Planet being caught her attention. His eyes narrowed as he followed her movements. His focus on her caused her to feel anxious.

∞-Most High Elected,-∞ Dahi's thoughts came tumbling into her head. She heard his thoughts through the consul in the transportation disc.

Rohongra stilled. ∞-I am waiting for your testimony. Have you arrived?-∞ Never before had she wished to be in his presence, to see his countenance like she did now, to see the damage to her planet through him. It angered her that duty had pulled until she felt only she could be the one to handle the Water Planet beings. If only Dahi and Ka did not think of them as Disposables, then she could have been the one who had raced to help her people.

∞-There is nothing.-∞ His thoughts accused. ∞-None exist after the blast.-∞

Rohongra's breath caught. She fought the closing and gasped several times. The others from her planet watched, but did not approach. She swirled in a circle panting. ∞-None? How can that be?-∞ Her garment collapsed in folds as she fell to the planet floor. ∞-We left transportation discs! Surely some have made it to safety,-∞ she argued.

∞-None that I have found. The Beings who came with me are angry. They blame you for the loss of life. Loss of consciousness and their home. You and your greed.-∞

She searched the countenance of those from her planet that surrounded her. Did they believe this was true as well?

Rohongra shook her head. ∞-It was not my greed that caused this! I never wanted to open the cavern to the middle planet. You came up with that idea. You and Ka! You felt the Duji embedded there was stronger, more valuable-∞

∞-You were the leader. A weak and foolish one at that. Like your father. You must be held accountable for your acts.-∞

The dust beneath her stirred and her limbs swept the air. She accepted a portion of the blame. She never should have kept Dahi as her thought leader. His ties with Ka and Celute intertwined. How her father had kept him all those years, she had no idea. ∞-I must meet with my Beings immediately. Make clear what has happened. Offer my sorrow to them.-∞

∞-Your sorrow will not save us.-∞ Dahi snorted. ∞-Nor will your thoughts. Without the Duji from ThAak-Too the galaxy will once again be at war. All of the Beings in the Astral Zone will know it is because of you.-∞

Dahi's public thoughts caused the Beings surrounding her to one by one vanish inside the transportation disc. Soon Rohongra saw some of the Hu-Mans, the few who had been in

84

line waiting to disembark, pushed toward her. They were shoved and pulled out of the ship and left to congregate around her in confusion.

She felt the young Hu-Mans' eyes accuse her too.

∞-I must . . . I must.-∞ Her thoughts betrayed her and she could not complete them.

The transportation disc, rose from the planet and vanished in the clouds. Her Beings had lost faith and left her to whatever fate the Yon-Ya's would devise.

∞-No! This cannot be.-∞

∞-Our remaining Beings and I will await you on Celute. Ka has given his permission for us to stay there. Come and plead your case in front of the Most High Council one last time, before you become Most High no more.-∞ Dahi's thoughts, still connected to the departing ship came to her.

Rohongra closed her thoughts and bowed her head. What was she to do?

The Hu-Mans parted as the Most High Council of Yon-Ya hurried toward her.

∞-We have listened to your thoughts. You must leave immediately,-∞ a Yon-Ya informed her. ∞-You landing here places us in great danger.-∞

Her throat issued a cough. ∞-I cannot now.-∞ Her limb pointed to the stars.

The Yon-Yas handled her roughly as they lifted her from the planet floor. Dust drifted from her covering to the ground. ∞-Most High Bodha will deal with you upon his return. Until then you will gather with these beings you have brought unauthorized to our planet.-∞

Rohongra cringed. Her innermost space was filled with pain. She touched the spot on her chest and released her emotions. She sensed the discomfort of the Yon-Yas.

∞-We are a peaceful planet. We cannot be caught between a war again. You will prepare to leave when our Most

High Bodha returns.-∞ The face that had originally greeted her with compassion, closed its thoughts to her.

Rohongra felt incredibly separated from all she had known, as if a cloak of seclusion had draped her being.

Rohongra still could not believe she had been left on the planet of Yon-Ya by her Beings - abandoned on a strange world with even stranger Beings surrounding her. Wetness silkened her face. She placed her limbs over her head and floated, trying to feel the security of being one with the universe.

She sensed the Hu-Mans gathered around her moving away. Only one stayed beside her. She tried to enter his thoughts, but they were closed to her or empty. She sank once more to the dust.

∞-Most High?-∞

Rohongra saw the Yon-Ya council gathered around her. She rose and lifted her Being as high as she could. Their decision would seal her fate. She knew she'd violated the treaty and her life force could be lost.

∞-We have been unable to contact Most High Bodha and are fearful what this may mean. As we have said, we are peaceful Beings and wish no harm, but cannot allow this situation. Our Most High assured us no Hu-Mans from the Water Planet would be allowed to enter our space, nor land on our world. We felt this would protect us from Ka and those who might choose affray.-∞ Rohongra knew they referred indirectly to her planet. All knew of the alliance between Celute and ThAak-Too. ∞-We are most aggrieved to have you and your Beings bring the Hu-Mans to our planet. Most distressed your planet has met a disastrous end, and so many of your Beings have become no more. Yet, we cannot allow you and these life forces to wander our home.-∞

Rohongra's head bowed. She acknowledged their thoughts. If she were to lose life force, she would do so without begging for mercy.

The Being in front of her gasped. ∞-No! We do not have common thought. We are removing you and the Hu-Mans to the wall. There you will remain until Most High Bodha returns or Most High Elected Soluma-Rah removes you. Prepare immediately.-∞

Rohongra turned to study the wall in the distance. High spiking hills blocked her view to the land beyond.

∞-There will be enough to sustain you inside the valley for however long it takes, but there is only one way in and out. I shall warn you, we will guard it and remove life force from any who attempt to leave.-∞

∞-I am most humbled by your choice to assist us.-∞

The Beings from Yon-Ya gathered the Hu-Mans and, by pointing, moved them toward the mountain wall. They seemed to be willing to go. She sensed some of their fright, but several provided encouragement as they walked. Rohongra guessed less than one hundred of the Hu-Mans had been waiting on the ramp and been left with her. She didn't think Dahi would cause war over such an insignificant number, but he might to get to her and remove her from power.

As the entire group gained elevation, she noticed some of the Hu-Mans became weak. It pleased her when the older ones lifted the younger and continued. She hoped to not give the Yon-Ya's any reason to change their collective mind.

Even while they moved increasingly higher, the wall towered over her and her Hu-Man charges. Behind, she felt the council follow. The Beings were going to ensure all of them went easily into the space beyond.

Rohongra marveled at the beauty of the land of Yon-Ya, so different from her own flat and dusty home. She looked up at the star they all connected with and felt warmed, not baked by its light. One from Yon-Ya led them when they reached the wall. They would now travel in single file on a narrow path. The rest of the Yon-Ya's waited at the edge and would go no further. Rohongra allowed the Hu-Mans to go first.

She turned to address the Beings from the ledge above them. ∞-Most High Rohongra from the planet ThAak-Too is grateful and indebted to your Beings.-∞ She bowed once and then disappeared from their view around a corner of the mountain wall.

Several more steps brought her to the place where the remaining Yon-Ya waited. All of the Hu-Mans had already slipped through a narrow opening.

∞-Most High, I am to inform you someone will guard this place. You and the Hu-Mans must not try to leave or we will take action. I wish you well.-∞

Rohongra slipped between the rocks. As her limbs touched the hardness around her, she felt its moisture. She moved easily through and stepped out on the other side. The Hu-Mans waited just outside the mouth of the wall. Tall, spiky landmasses surrounded them. There appeared to be truly only one way in or out of the valley. She moved to the left and around the Hu-Mans. The ground beneath her feet was as a sponge. Each step lifted her and she sprang lightly. Burrows grew around her and she reached over, pulled a piece off and slipped it into her mouth, savoring the sweet taste. ∞-At least they wouldn't starve.-∞

The Hu-Man, who had watched her closely before, stepped beside her, reached up and grabbed a burrow. He bit into it and chewed. Quickly he grabbed several more and handed them to the others. She touched his arm with her limb. ∞-Only one each. No more or you will feel pain later,-∞ she advised. She heard his voice and the others obeyed. She led them farther into the valley. They passed large towering roeds that would later provide them with shelter. Still she moved forward until she found a sparkling pool, iridescent in the starlight. She walked to the edge and stopped. The Hu-Man leader stood beside her. He

88

reached down with a cupped limb and tried to pull the moisture away.

Rohongra's Being filled with joyful surprise. She touched him. ∞-It cannot be removed from its center,-∞ she thought to him. ∞-Watch.-∞ Rohongra walked straight into the pool and immersed her Being. She felt the moisture enter her. With her thirst quenched, she rose. The Hu-Mans watched from the edge of the pool, nervous. She left the pool and reached for the leader. ∞-Come in,-∞ she instructed. ∞-I will show you.-∞

The Hu-Man walked into the pool with her. She placed her limb over his face and immersed him. He fought her. ∞-Relax, the moisture will fill you.-∞ When she sensed his understanding, she released him.

He rose from the pool and used his voice to call to the others.

Rohongra left the Hu-Mans and returned to the roeds. Starlight would not shine much longer. She stood beneath them one at a time and shook them. Blossoms floated to the ground, covering it with soft down.

The Hu-Man watched. Then his thoughts found hers. ∞-What do you think will happen when Most High Bodha returns?-∞

∞-He is a Being of peace. He will remove you and your beings to a safe place. Me, well, I may be a risk.-∞

∞-Does that not worry you? Don't you wish to flee? To get to safety?-∞

∞-I have no way to flee. Nowhere to go. But I have faith in Most High Bodha's goodness. I have sat in many councils with him.-∞

The Hu-Man looked to the ground. ∞-Is this where we will sleep?-∞

∞-Yes, starlight will be gone very soon. This is where we will rest.-∞

The Hu-Man nodded and left her to return to the others at the pool. It was only then Rohongra realized she had not touched him, nor he her, during their thought transfer.

Chapter 14

Mandy worked on her hands and knees pulling weeds in the agriculture center. She couldn't believe how good Evan smelled even though they had been in the Biosphere for more than two weeks. She was positive that she did not smell that good. She went back to observing him and tried to push her stench out of her mind. His strong arms moved next to her. She felt drawn to Evan, because he was incredibly smart and reminded her of Jesse, the good-looking guy who joined her brother and her for the short drive before he was taken by aliens.

He worked quickly, pulling twice the weeds she did. He inspected the greenery for new insects, threw the weeds into a pile when he found none, and moved on to the next. He picked up a bug, and studied it with quiet concentration. He wrote down notes on a clipboard. Then he leaned over, grab the next handful and continued his methodical weed pulling. Evan and Mandy worked in silence, but it bugged her. Finally the silence overwhelmed her and she asked the first question that came to mind.

"How did you end up here?" she asked.

"I came a few months back for an internship in entomology. Bugs."

"Why? I mean, why here?"

"My father encouraged me to come. I always knew I wanted to work with plants." He shrugged. "I wanted to stay close to home, near family, but . . ." Evan cleared his throat. "Well, whenever my mother and father actually came together on a subject, which didn't happen often, they had the power of persuasion on their side. There was no discussion."

Mandy lowered her voice. "Do you miss them?" Immediately she saw him tense. "I'm sorry."

Evan sat back on his heels, his eyes focused on his hands. "I thought I'd be gone for a year. Now, my mother is gone and I have no idea if I'll ever see anyone else again."

Mandy noticed the skin on his neck become splotchy. He blinked. She swallowed a lump. "Are we going to be okay?"

"We should get back to work," Evan said. He picked up a weed, and seemed to look at a tiny green bug clinging to life and a leaf. Mandy studied the tiny creature's movement along the edge. Charlie stepped closer and appeared to break Evan's concentration in the process. Charlie sniffed the air and Evan turned toward Mandy. He opened his mouth to say something, but words never came out.

"She's not going to hurt your plants, Evan." Mandy quickly defended Charlie. "See how she moves around them? She can sense how important they are to you."

Evan shifted his weight to the left and closer to Mandy. His arm brushed a plant Mandy reached for. Charlie moved away, and then turned circles for a moment before lying down.

"How long do you think we'll be in here?" Evan asked. "Do you think we'll ever be able to leave? That we'll find others who've survived?" His eyes were red.

Mandy pushed a tentative smile to her lips. "Of course, there are others. I'm sure your father, brothers and grandmother are all just waiting out the ash cloud."

"Scientists predicted if this occurred it would be years before the Earth could sustain life again."

"Scientists have been wrong before, haven't they?" She didn't wait for his answer. Instead she said, "You know what I'm going to do when this is all over? I'm going to kick some alien butt to get my brother back. It was all a giant lie. The aliens weren't here to save us. They didn't help. Those stupid, weird looking things took my brother and left me behind. Like I'm not good enough to live on their planet." Evan's green eyes stared through her.

"Oh?" he said.

Mandy nodded. "Yep, that is what I'm going to do. Find my brother and catch those no good aliens."

Charlie stood. Her hackles rose and a low growl came from deep within her throat. Evan reared back.

"What's wrong, girl?" Mandy rubbed her fur, but Charlie's eyes stayed focused on the roof.

Evan and Mandy looked up. Phillip rushed past them. He moved quickly, but silently. Mandy jumped out of his way.

"What's wrong?" she asked.

Phillip put his finger to his lips, not slowing down a bit, he moved through the agriculture area and up the walkway to the kitchen. Evan and Mandy looked at each other. Neither moved.

"Something is wrong," Mandy whispered. She knelt beside Charlie, her arms around the dog's neck.

"Do you think it's people? Or the aliens? I mean, would they come back to take more people?" Evan quivered next to her.

Mandy turned to him, her eyes wide. Tears formed and rolled down her face. Oh, no. What if aliens had come to get her? To get them all?

Evan reached an arm around her. "I'm sorry. How stupid. It's probably nothing."

"It's not nothing," Mandy said. "Phillip doesn't move like that when it's nothing." She shivered. She knew they were in danger, but from what? "We should go find Francine and the others.

* * *

Dagny sat with Bolton standing beside her.

"So what do we do now, y'all?" Aspen paced along the dining table.

Dagny also wondered what they should do. When she'd first heard about the figures on the roof, her heart wouldn't stop racing. People? Or were they aliens. Mandy had said the aliens had tracked her brother and their friend. Maybe they were looking for more recruits. So far Phillip hadn't said a word, and he would have been the one to know for sure. Dagny's eyes narrowed. She smeared butter on a slice of bread and stuffed it in her mouth. Food always made a stressful situation better.

Bolton shook his head. His gaze lowered to focus on Dagny briefly, she didn't know if it was in response to Aspen's question or a condemnation of her eating. Gently she placed the rest of the offending bread on her plate and wiped her hands on her pants. Dang. They needed to eat the food. It would just rot otherwise.

"Where's Phillip now?" Bolton demanded. His hand rubbed the back of his neck.

"He went back outside," Francine said. She sat at the head of the table, her hands folded in front of her. "And Mandy and Evan are in the garden. "

"The Agricultural Center or IAB," Aspen corrected.

"He's outside!" Bolton pounded on the table and Dagny jumped, as did her bread. "Why did you let him go out again? We almost had an incident and he's gone back outside? If anything we should be working to make the Biosphere more secure."

"Set yourself down," Aspen said, her voice steel. "He went out there to begin with 'cause of the fires. And he needed to go back out to make sure those people. . ."

"Or aliens," Dagny interjected.

"Fine, or aliens, had gone and the fire is not threatenin' us," Aspen said.

94

Dagny got the distinct impression Aspen inferred that Bolton was less of a man for not going out as well. "Don't talk to Doctor Bolton that way." She began to rise to her feet.

Bolton shook his head and sat. "I can't believe you're okay with this, Francine. You should know how important it is we keep our group safe."

Dagny stared at the bread on her plate, it seemed Aspen's words and attitude meant nothing to him. Francine didn't respond.

"He said he saw five people?" Bolton asked a bit more calmly.

"People or aliens? Dagny asked.

Bolton rolled his eyes. "Could he tell anything about the things he saw?"

Francine leaned forward, her elbows on the table. "He said he saw shadows. It appeared there were five and when they turned to climb the dome, he thought they had weapons, but he couldn't be sure."

"I can't believe they climbed the dome. How deep is that ash anyway?" Dagny said hoping to get Bolton's attention.

"Phillip said the drifting ash is ten feet deep in some places. So, apparently the whole Biosphere looks more like a hill. We should be happy they crossed where they did," Francine said, "otherwise they might have been able to see into the rainforest. There is little ash covering that area for some reason."

"Y'all could someone see our lights?" Aspen asked.

"Phillip says the ash is still really thick in the air so it's hard to see anything. Which is why those people walked so close to him before he noticed them."

"Ah can't believe the roof is holdin' up. That's what surprises me."

They nodded around the table. Dagny cast a surreptitious look at her bread.

"It's apparent the dome is able to hold the additional weight of the ash turned cement." Bolton's hands, folded on the table, seemed to mean he felt placated, but Dagny noticed his knuckles were white. "So what are we going to do about it?" He glared at Francine, a false grin pasted to his face.

"We're going to wait and see what Phillip says when he returns," she declared.

Bolton exhaled loudly. "And what if there are others. Sooner or later someone is going to walk over the rainforest and notice what's going on in here. Then what? We can't sit around waiting. We need to do something." Bolton stood.

"Like what?" Aspen asked.

"I've been working on the two-way radio," Dagny offered. "Phillip's been helping and we think we've almost got it fixed."

"That's great," Francine said.

Bolton clapped his hands. "Really? We want to evade other groups, not commune with them. Doesn't anyone understand what I'm talking about? We've got a sweet deal here and we're going to blow it."

"Those could be people who need our help," Francine said.

"Or they could be aliens or other people who will eat our food and kill us off," Bolton retorted.

"Then it's probably a good idea we get the radio working," Dagny said. His gaze was firmly on her now. "Well, I thought it would help. Knowing what's going on out there and all." She licked her lips. Dagny smiled as a thought occurred. "I really could use some help, some guidance. Doctor Bolton, do you know anything about radios?" She blinked rapidly.

Bolton frowned. "Not a thing."

"Perhaps you should give it a look," Francine said. "Dagny, take the doctor to the technology center and see if he

96

can help you get the radio working. We need to know what's happening out there. There are probably others like us all over."

"Come on, Doctor." Dagny rose. She gave one last look at her bread and led him away.

"So what is the problem with the radio, anyway?" he asked as he followed her down the hallway.

"Some of the wires were unconnected. Phillip, though, thinks he has everything back together again."

"I must admit to you, I know nothing of this sort of thing."

"That's okay." Dagny stopped, turned and grabbed his arm with both hands. "I'll teach you."

Chapter 15

Evan stood at the base of a tree in the rainforest and waited patiently for Doc to mumble, "go." Days had gone by and still no decision had been made regarding what to do about the roof over the rainforest. He had to admit he didn't like the situation any more than Mandy. The people who had trespassed on the roof days earlier had apparently not posed enough of a threat, and so their little group had put off making a rash decision. But already, they had guessed, two to three more groups had also passed by. Instead of coming up with a solution to the rainforest issue, they all passed the time focusing on other things. His favorite was the one he and Mandy were getting ready to play.

He meant to give Mandy a five second head start up the tree, even though she said she didn't want any special treatment. He'd be surprised if she won, but he knew once you were up the banana tree, anything could happen. They had created this fun little activity to pass the time; whoever lost would be doing the other one's morning chores, and it kept them in bananas too. Evan was excited because on the last banana race he turned over laundry duty to Aspen for a week. In order to win, he had to pick a banana and make it back down the tree before the other contestant.

"Go."

Evan heard Mandy scurrying up the tree before his brain came out of wandering mode and kicked in.

He scrambled to catch up. Evan laughed; she might beat him after all. But that would be okay with him; it would mean he'd have extra chores in the Agriculture Center with Aspen.

With all the crops ready to harvest, everyone needed to take shifts. He actually considered slowing down his speed. Mandy, though, would assume he'd let her win. She didn't believe she could win unless he cheated. Decisions, decisions. He didn't want to hurt Mandy's feelings. She had become the one girl he could talk to without stuttering.

"Hey Mandy, I gave you a head start but I don't think that's going to help you much," Evan teased.

Evan could hear Doc down below mumbling about the ridiculousness of play. "Come on. Move it. I'm hungry."

The bananas were going to be used for a breakfast shake.

"Maybe, Doc if you had more fun…" Evan called down to him.

Charlie, growling low in the back of her throat, cut off Evan's sentence. "Get the lights," Evan said as he jumped down. The rainforest went pitch black. He found Mandy on the ground at the base of her tree.

"Are you okay?" he whispered.

She nodded. Charlie paced next to her. They backed up to join Doc by the circuit breakers.

"Do you think we got the lights off in time?" Evan asked.

"Not sure. I don't hear or see anything," Doc said. "You sure this is what that growl from Charlie meant? Maybe, she just has to excrete or something."

"I'm positive," Mandy said. "It's the only time I've ever heard her growl like that."

Evan could see Mandy's knees tremble and her hands shake. "It's okay. They probably won't even get close. And we got the light out."

"Phillip doesn't know for sure who or what keeps trespassing over the roof," Mandy softly spoke. She exhaled.

Evan held his breath and waited. Mandy had said she was certain they were aliens, and he didn't know exactly how he felt about that. The last time when they'd had to turn out the lights, the two of them had huddled on the floor of the agricultural center for close to an hour talking about family. She had shared with him everything and he found himself telling her stories about his family as well. He knew she was scared, and tired of hiding while the group mulled over what to do.

Doc bumped into him and knocked Evan out of his reverie. They were at tremendous risk to be seen. The only spot of the roof completely free of ash was over the rainforest where they hid in the shadows. Minutes ticked by, nothing happened. Doc shifted from foot to foot, as he clenched and unclenched his fists. "This is stupid. That dog doesn't know what it's doing. We need to get back to work. I'm turning on the lights."

Mandy looked up at Evan, a plea of some sort in her eyes.

"Doc, you don't want to do that," Evan whispered. "Let's wait just a bit more."

"I'm tired, hungry and I don't enjoy standing in the dark. I'm turning on the lights, grabbing the bananas and going to make breakfast."

Charlie's growl increased with intensity, but remained low in the back of her throat. Evan couldn't see well, but felt sure Doc had his hand on the breaker.

"Don't," Evan whispered as loud as he dared.

Seconds, felt like minutes. Across the roof appeared shadows. Evan sucked in air. He realized Charlie, who stood between him and Mandy, had stopped growling. They stood perfectly quiet. Shadows crisscrossed the roof. One stopped, Mandy put her hand over her mouth. He prayed she could control her scream. He prayed he could as well.

Phillip stepped beside them, coming out of nowhere. Both Evan and Mandy jumped, but luckily Doc only gasped. Phillip stared intently at the ceiling.

100

Finally, the feet above them moved. As they journeyed across the roof and away from the open area, Charlie began to growl again. Then finally she stopped. Pushing her head under Mandy's hand, she waited for her reward.

"Stupid dog almost got us killed." Doc seethed.

"No, she didn't. In fact, she probably saved you," Phillip said.

"Phillip's right," Evan piped in. "She gave us enough warning to turn off the lights, then remained quiet until they were far enough away not to hear. And when there was no longer a threat, she let us know. She saved us. Good dog." He reached over and gave her a pat.

"Well she's a high-cost warning system. She eats a ton and she has big piles of waste that produce CO_2," Doc said.

"Those piles of waste are what keeps the garden growing, Doc," Evan told him.

"Bolton, you're just mad, because one time that pile of waste landed in your shoe," Phillip said.

"Good girl. Thanks for the warning," Mandy told her.

Doc turned on his heel and stomped out.

"You know I'm right," Evan said.

"Yeah, yeah," Doc mumbled, his back still turned.

"Good girl, Charlie." Evan scratched behind her ears. "Good girl indeed." Evan laughed. Soon all three had tears flowing from their eyes.

* * *

Later that day Mandy stepped into the dining room where everyone sat around the table. She had learned to appreciate and respect the group; each person worked to keep everything up and running. Mandy smiled despite the tenseness of the situation. Charlie sat, licked her chops and let drool drip to the floor. Thankfully, the doctor ranted and drew attention away from her. He said something about being 'proactive' with the people on the roof.

"Can I get…?" Mandy stopped. Francine set a plate of food in front of her. She wanted to share with Charlie, but a dish with scraps already sat on the floor.

"Look, we need to focus here. We won't survive if we aren't careful. This is the fourth time people have wandered over the area. We need to shut off the lights in the rainforest. I know it wouldn't be easy for them to walk right over it, but eventually someone will notice the light and climb over to see what's inside. It's the only spot not covered by ash. Anyone can look in," Doc spat.

"We can't. The trees will die. Then they'll produce too much carbon," Evan said.

"We have other plants. Can't they balance out the system?" Doc persevered.

Evan shook his head and made a strange guttural sound.

"It's too much of a risk," Francine stated.

Mandy thought Francine tried really hard to mediate the situation.

"Well, do you have a better idea?" Bolton turned to Francine and said in his, I'm talking to such infantile children here, tone. Mandy hated when he did that. "At anytime more people could wander over the top of us. We're too exposed."

Ever since the first time, when she was with Evan in the agricultural area, Mandy had found herself looking up and listening. Not that she'd ever heard a thing, she just felt watched. It might be silly or it might be aliens with x-ray vision. She didn't know.

So Mandy understood Doc's position, but she didn't think yelling at people would help get anything done. They worked well as a team and that was what she thought they needed now – everyone coming together to work out a solution. Not a grown man acting like an idiot every chance he got. She

102

hoped Francine would stop him soon. She seemed to have a way of calming him down, or at least making him so mad he left the room, which allowed a productive conversation to occur.

Charlie slurped next to Mandy, momentarily interrupting her thoughts. She reached down to pet the top of her head. Charlie was all she had left. She blinked several times. "We're not actually sure they're humans. They could be aliens for all we know, looking to snatch more people," Mandy said.

Doc gave her a disgusted glance.

"Why can't we relocate ash to cover that spot?" Evan asked.

"The wind is too strong. It would blow the ash away," Phillip said.

"Well, why don't we cover it with a tarp?" Francine asked.

"That's a good idea. Can we do it y'all? Should it be on the outside or the inside?" Aspen asked.

"Someone might notice if it's on the outside. But it would be much more difficult to get it on the ceiling inside," Evan said.

"I agree, it would be easier from the outside," Doc stated.

"Way too dangerous. Someone could blow off the roof. It's a twenty-foot drop. If you fell that far, you'd get seriously injured," Phillip informed them.

"I'm not risking my life for a tarp," stammered Dagny.

"Then let's do it from inside, y'all." Everyone stared at Aspen.

Mandy thought she might have an idea of how to do it, but was done with having her thoughts shot down. She sat quietly and watched Dagny, her face white and her hands shook when she picked up her water glass.

"That's the best option. I'll find a tarp, make an adhesive, so it will stick to the roof and some clamps for reinforcement.

Evan, can you dig out the ladder from the closet behind the rainforest? It's an extension ladder and should be able to reach the roof," Phillip said.

"Do we have everything you'll need?" Doc asked.

"I'll start working on it." Phillip looked over at Mandy. Problem solved Mandy thought. Well almost. Unless the individuals on the roof were aliens and not people, in that case, Mandy didn't think a tarp over a hole would protect them. With a solution in place and dinner done, the group got to work.

Mandy was put in charge of gathering some of the supplies. She rushed into the rainforest with her list of items. She had to find all the rope she could, to tie into the holes around the outside of the tarp, but before she did that, she wanted one last look at the dark space above her head where the stars used to be. After they placed the cover, she'd lose even that small comfort.

Charlie barked at an animal hidden in the shadows. Mandy absently patted her head. She wished she could see the brilliant light from twinklers once more. That's what her dad had called the stars. Mandy blinked several times. Her father always said the stars looked like firecrackers in the sky. Anytime she saw them she thought of him, a firecracker that never quit. She could no longer hold the tears back.

Charlie nudged Mandy's hand. "I'm okay girl," she said. They walked towards the mountain conveniently planted in the middle of the rainforest. It lay covered in trees and had a two-fold purpose. It created a higher ground for the Gallegos to hide in and contained a natural looking storage unit. Underneath, hidden away, lay buckets, ladders, cutting shears and other tools.

Mandy and Charlie climbed to the top of the waterfall. She worried about the Gallegos. She'd never seen them, even though she'd been living in the Biosphere for weeks. The Gallegos spent their time hiding in the trees or the thick underbrush. Occasionally, Charlie would hear them, so somehow they found nutrition and shelter.

104

"I miss my mom and dad," she said to Charlie, scratching behind her ears. Charlie barked and more animals seemed to scurry out of the way. "And I hope Derek and Jesse are okay."

"What?" Evan's voice startled her.

"Oh, uh, nothing," Mandy stammered. She turned away so she could wipe her face with her sleeve.

"I'm supposed to get the ladder. Phillip will be here soon," Evan said.

"I'll help." Mandy followed Evan off the hill and into the storage area.

"Do you believe in love at first sight?" Mandy asked.

"Um, maybe. I guess."

"What do you think about being in extreme danger and love? Do you think people's feelings are more intense?" Mandy looked up, as Evan turned away walking deeper into the hillside.

"What?"

"Well, I mean do you think being at risk makes people's feelings seem deeper. You know like because they're afraid to die alone, but not deep enough to sustain the feelings once that danger is over? Having someone has to be better than being alone, don't you think?"

Evan became still. She waited for an answer that never came.

"How would you know if it's true love?" she continued.

Evan moved to the left shoving items out of his way. He seemed to stiffen and glance at her sideways. "Not sure."

Sometimes he was so hard to communicate with. "How did you know you were in love with your girlfriend or in love for the first time?"

"Hey kid, do you hear someone coming?" Evan squirmed.

Mandy stopped moving so she could better listen. "No."

"Oh, well, I'm going to go find Doc or Phillip, yeah Phillip, and see if he um, needs help with the paste or glue or whatever. Can you finish looking for the ladder?" Evan shoved his hands into his pockets and ducked his head.

Mandy looked up to answer, but Evan had already left. So weird she thought. She went back to moving items around looking for the ladder, her mind still wandering to Jesse - the cute, blue-eyed, and blond haired Jesse, who joined them a few days before the eruption. When Mandy and her brother met him outside the gas station in Wyoming he'd planned to hunker down in the deep freeze and eat Twinkies until it was safe to come out. She bet he didn't know it would've been years before that could've happened.

He'd worn a cowboy hat and his voice sounded smooth like butter. When he joined them, before the aliens snatched him and her brother, she'd giggled when he spoke, and had butterflies in her stomach. She didn't know if love felt like that, but she had liked him and missed him now. He would have made this life without her family a bit more bearable.

Mandy located the ladder and carried it to the entrance of the storage area. She felt guilty Jesse had chosen to come with them. Especially as it only made him available when the aliens came. Now she wondered where he and her brother had been taken and if they were all right.

Charlie barked, "I know girl, I hear them." Mandy sighed and picked up the ladder.

* * *

Phillip carried a small bucket of adhesive from his shop to the rainforest. He felt lucky to have found everything he needed. He recalled as a kid, his mom making homemade glue for him and his brother. It took awhile, mixing and re-working certain substances before he got the exact recipe. He put together a concoction of gelatin, water, glycerin and a small amount of vinegar. He was pleased to find glycerin a common ingredient in shampoo and conditioner, so easily available even now. The rest of the items he found in the kitchen.

Phillip saw Evan walking quickly toward him. "Aren't we meeting in the rainforest?"

"Yeah, coming to find you. " Evan stood taller. "You have the adhesive?"

"Yep."

"Will it work?"

"Hope so. Need to cover ten-feet. Do we have the rope, the carabineers, and a knife?"

"Do we even have all that stuff?" Evan asked.

"I told Bolton where to find it. We use ropes and carabineers for maintaining the turbines occasionally."

Evan nodded and followed him. Phillip hoped they'd be able to pull it off. He figured he could stand on the sixteen-foot ladder and have Evan and Aspen each climb a tree. Bolton would stand on the metal structure used for maintenance of the trees, while Francine would be on the ground, helping to navigate each of them. Phillip calculated Mandy could walk up the side of the glass if Francine belayed her. Not sure how Dagny handled heights, he'd decided to keep her close to the ground. She would stand on a smaller ladder placed on the rainforest hill.

Now, he only had to run the plan past everyone, have Bolton shut-up and agree, put some rope and adhesive around the tarp, get it to stick to the dome ceiling and have everyone safely return to the ground. Piece of cake, he thought.

Evan and Phillip were the last to arrive. Bolton stood giving orders. Phillip placed the plastic down, ignoring him. He cut the rope, and tied it through the holes in the tarp. Mandy quickly caught on and helped. Soon, it seemed everyone else ignored Bolton as well.

"What's next Phillip?" Aspen asked.

"Smear adhesive all the way around." In no time they finished, and everyone stood in place ready to climb. The trick would be for them to ascend at the same speed, otherwise the tarp might get tangled.

"Mandy, you ready?" Phillip worried most about her. As the tiniest she would scale the side of the glass where small metal railings crisscrossed the windows. This made her the most vulnerable. "Francine, you hold onto her tight." They'd figured a way to loop a rope high over the dome and use it to keep Mandy from falling.

"I've got her, don't worry," Francine called to him.

"Start climbing, slow and steady."

He moved one foot up, then the next, careful not to drop the clamps that would be used to secure the tarp to the frame. Phillip's confidence in the plan increased. He heard a thump and stopped. "What happened?"

"It's okay. A monkey startled me," Evan yelled.

Phillip grunted. "You okay?"

"Fine."

"Need a moment to recover from the monkey attack?" Dagny laughed.

"Funny, no."

"Okay, let's keep going." Phillip moved up the ladder again. He hoped his body would hold out. It was a long way up. His knees weren't what they used to be. Charlie barked and Phillip heard animals around him scurry.

"Shut-up," Bolton yelled.

"Don't tell her to shut-up," Mandy retorted.

"That stupid dog is breaking my concentration. Shut-her up."

"Shush, Charlie, it's okay," Mandy told her.

"Should Charlie wait outside?" Francine asked.

"Y'all, we're too close to being finished."

108

"No, let's go back down," Phillip said. He felt the tarp descend and he moved at the same pace. Mandy reached the bottom, removed Charlie from the forest and then returned to her position before Phillip could catch his breath.

"Okay, we ready?" he asked.

Dagny revealed sweat-stained armpits. He guessed she didn't enjoy their task, but she didn't say anything. She walked up the mountain and repositioned herself. Everyone was in place. They began to ascend and gained momentum. In no time they were where they left off. Phillip reached the top, and held onto the frame with his left hand. He used his right to secure the tarp. After pushing on it for a few minutes, he slowly and steadily reached for the clip on his belt. He attempted to squeeze it open far enough to clamp down on the frame. He teetered backwards. Over correcting, he leaned forward and grabbed the frame with both hands. The clamp fell to the ground.

"Need help, Phillip?" Bolton asked sarcastically.

"I've got it." He reached for his other clamp and this time got it easily around the frame. The doctor's attitude could help motivate a bull to perfection, Phillip thought. He finished and climbed down. With his feet firmly planted on the ground, he walked over to where Mandy clutched the window frame about halfway up the dome.

"What's wrong?" he asked Francine.

"We had a little miss-hap, she swung out over the rain-forest. Enough to scare her."

"She get the clamps on?"

Francine nodded. "She just has to climb down."

"Mandy, focus, breathe, you can do this. Don't look at the ground. Move a little to the left. There's the perfect handhold. Good, now your foot. You got it," Evan called to her.

Everyone else joined Evan, Phillip and Francine to watch.

"Almost there. One more."

Mandy jumped from the ledge. Her face was pale and she had beads of sweat on her upper lip. She touched the ground.

"Good job."

She smiled at Phillip. "Thanks."

"I wonder what it looks like from the outside?" Bolton asked.

"Go check it out. Let me know," Phillip said. He chuckled as he walked away. Thankful, no one had been injured and the tarp held secure, at least for now.

Chapter 16

∞

The Most High Elected, Ka of Celute, landed home and issued orders to those around him. ∞-Remove the Disposables to their habitat at once.-∞

His round torso and short limbs caused him to waddle as he made his way down the ship's ramp, his most precious, Omis, glided elegantly beside him. Her head touched his, the downy white hair gentle on his face.

∞-Your plans take shape,-∞ she thought.

Ka's face spread. ∞-Yes. All comes together.-∞

∞-Is it a problem we will have no Duji now?-∞ Omis had long ago left her husband and daughter to join with those of Celute. While her skin had faded, her long limbs and appendages showed her true origin.

∞-We shall have need to search the galaxy for another source of power. Do not worry, beloved. Our source of Polisis is great, as is our wealth in Disposables. When war comes, and it surely will, we shall survive.-∞

∞-I'm more concerned for the cold nights,-∞ she retorted.

∞-Our Polisis is still desired. Foolish Beings will give up their power to receive it. They will steal it from their neighbor to get it.-∞ Ka snorted. ∞-Of all the Astral Zone, we shall be fine.-∞

∞-And what of my dear friend, Dahi? What shall we do with him?-∞

Ka patted her limb where it lay across his chest. ∞-Oh, no worries, my precious. He shall be dealt with.-∞

Ka and Omis stopped and watched as the Hu-Man Disposables were herded into their pen. Some still fought off the gas used to induce rest. They stumbled and fell and were quickly stepped on by those behind. He shook his large head. ∞-Do not allow damage to come to my workers,-∞ he thought. The Celutes, who herded, slowed down and became more careful. None wished to cross their Most High.

∞-Ka, I am honored to be the first to welcome you home.-∞ Dahi approached reclining on a feather soft cushion carried by twelve ThAak-Toons.

∞-You know it is an act of war between our planets for you to be here?-∞ Ka's eyes narrowed. He removed Omis's limb from where it rested and stepped in front of her. ∞-You presume too much. You and your Beings.-∞

Dahi shrank deeper in the cushion. ∞-I am so very sorry, Most High. I did not think . . . We have always been in accord.-∞

∞-Yes, we have. When you had something I needed and wished for, Duji. Now you have nothing.-∞ Ka shared a chuckle with Omis. ∞-So you have no reason to be in my presence. I am sure Soluma-Rah will find you a nice home. Come precious. I am starved.-∞

∞-Wait,-∞ Dahi pleaded. ∞-Perhaps I still have something you want.-∞

Ka stepped close. ∞-And what would that be?-∞

∞-Rohongra and the Hu-Mans she carries in her holds.-∞

Ka tilted his head. ∞-What use do I have for more Hu-Mans?-∞

∞-We both know your Disposables have a short life span. Not only do I know where Rohongra has hers, I also know how to get her to tell where Most High Bodha is hiding his. And make no mistake. The galaxy will turn to war without Duji.-∞

Ka was thoughtful. ∞-You think, but I have yet to see proof of what you endorse.-∞

112

∞-The ship is on its way. You will have proof in a few ektons.-∞

Ka and Omis continued to their home.

∞-Do you suppose our offspring will enjoy the new Disposables? Perhaps they could begin training them for war.-∞ Omis thought to Ka.

∞-We are aligned as one,-∞ Ka agreed.

* * *

Most High Bodha watched as his Beings opened the chambers one at a time and released the Water Planet beings from the bowels of the transportation disc. He placed his robes around him before he exited the tiny ship. Many Hu-Mans, still groggy from the fog used to calm and sedate them on their long voyage, veered and stumbled, but soon seemed to regain their balance. He felt pleasure to see the older beings help the younger ones as they descended onto the planet, Terrat.

∞-How soon before all will be evacuated and we can be on our way?-∞ Momur's thoughts intruded.

Bodha turned to his second. ∞-All are proceeding forward. It is going well.-∞

∞-We have heard more pleas from Yon-Ya through Ora-j. The council is demanding our whereabouts. ThAak-Toons have landed. They are concerned.-∞

∞-We shall soon return home.-∞ Bodha's gaze returned to the Hu-Mans. He noticed several of the offspring held small devices in their hands and walked around holding them into the sky. What were they doing? Their foreheads creased and their lips trembled.

∞-Are those devices of communication?-∞ he thought.

Momur swirled closer to observe the scene below them. ∞-They cannot communicate. Ka will find them and our fates will be sealed.-∞

113

∞-Easy, Momur. Their communication devices are useless. They do not have the technology. They will be safe here.-∞

∞-I worry more for us. What if Ka finds them?-∞ Momur shuddered. "Finds us?"

Bodha's thoughts turned inward. As much as he wanted to believe Ka would cause no more troubles, he knew that to be untrue. All accepted Ka wanted to be Supreme Most High, and none doubted he would do all within his power to accomplish this goal.

As Bodha watched the Hu-Mans, he became concerned. He sensed a sudden change. The younger ones wandered alone while the oldest ones seemed to be in conflict.

Momur touched his limb and pointed to a large group that swelled closer together before drawing apart. In the center, two young Hu-Mans whirled and joined in combat. Red flew from orifices and spattered Terrat.

∞-All are unloaded,-∞ a member of his crew informed Bodha.

Momur's eyes found his. ∞-They are not our concern. We should leave. They will figure out what to do. How to work together.-∞

Anguish filled Bodha's central Being. ∞-Bring the twelve strongest to council.-∞

Momur waited for the crewmember to leave before he questioned his Most High. ∞-We do not have time for this. I have been in agreement with your intentions all along, but this is too much. You risk us all. The longer we delay, the greater the risk to our Beings. The greater the risk to Yon-Ya.-∞ He pointed out the viewing space of the ship to the Hu-Mans. ∞-The risk to them.-∞

Bodha's head bowed. ∞-I cannot leave yet. My thoughts are one with the Most High Council. We agreed to not cause harm to the Hu-Mans.-∞

114

∞-It is not us that harms. It is they that harm each other. We cannot be held responsible.-∞

∞-But we are. We have brought them here and have given them no guidance.-∞

Soon after Bodha entered the council room and observed each of the twelve Hu-Man offspring and the Yon-Ya guard paired with them. He felt incredible sadness. The Hu-Man's thoughts merged with his and created chaos. Their thoughts all jumbled at once into his mind. They had no understanding of what pain their emotions caused him. He remained too close, and their thoughts, full of fear, were a powerful force. He fought to quiet them with his mind and help them choose Ten-Dati before he finally realized the futility and vocalized. While they quieted, some of their thoughts still rampaged in his mind. He finally discerned why they hurt each other. He sensed the fear they had and their inability to communicate in the same language.

∞-Please translate,-∞ Bodha announced to the guards, his vocal apparatus too weak to continue.

He waited until each of his Beings laid a hand on the Hu-Man in front of them. The thoughts quieted.

∞-This will be your new home. It is a safe place where your kind will begin again. Work together to become one with each other. There is safety here.-∞

∞-We need food, shelter and water. How can we survive here?-∞ The thought came and Bodha turned and acknowledged the Hu-Man who questioned well.

∞-This planet is much similar to yours. The fluid you seek can be found in the outpourings that flow from the green heart. It will quench your thirst and give you nutrition. Life blooms around to sustain you. You must seek your place of safety. I have chosen this world as it has few life forces that can cause you harm.-∞

∞-Few?-∞ The wariness of their thoughts invaded his mind again.

Bodha continued to be in turmoil and he struggled to calm his Being. The Most High Council had agreed to remove and relocate the youngest of the Hu-Mans and now these creatures had no preparation for their new future. He sensed that to leave them on Terrat without the appropriate instruction would mean their demise. His thoughts grew still. His gaze returned to the planet floor. Still the remaining Hu-Mans wandered, unable to unite.

He could sense Momur holding back. Could sense the Hu-Man fear in the room. Resigned he turned back to those in the council chamber. ∞-We shall divide your beings into twelve groups. Those groups will be instructed by my Beings for a period of time no more than five ektons on how to survive in your new home. You will decrease all anger and hatred for each other and instead work together in these groups to build your world.-∞

Bodha nodded, his thoughts were complete. All could leave now. He waited while the Hu-Mans and their translators vacated their positions. When he turned to Momur, his Being filled with sadness to see Momur had also removed himself.

116

Chapter 17

"Sit," Bolton told her. He kept one eye on the brut, Charlie. The medical center would need to be fully cleaned of dog hair again after they left.

"So explain to me why I have to see you again?" Mandy asked. She sat on the end of the patient bed in the medical center.

"You must be checked regularly the same as everyone else."

"Why? What difference does it make?"

"Even though it appears all is well, our health can take a deadly turn quite rapidly in this type of environment. We must stay on top of what is happening with our bodies, so we can counteract any issues before they affect us all. How is your arm?"

"Completely healed, but I'm not a fan of needles. I hate that you keep sticking me."

"It's protocol."

Bolton watched as Charlie, after sniffing every corner, found her way back to her master and sat.

"I wish you didn't always bring your dog. Can't Aspen keep her while we do this?"

"Why don't you check Charlie, too?"

"That's not my expertise." Charlie's eyes watched every move he made. "She makes me nervous. I worry she could bite," he said.

"Oh, no," Mandy said. "But of course, I don't really know her that well. I found her only a few days before I arrived here. So we've known each other weeks."

Bolton, who had been ready to take her blood, stopped. "Perhaps it'd be best if she waited for you outside?"

"She won't leave me now." Mandy smiled. "In fact, she'd probably break down a door to get to me."

Bolton eyed the door, and then the dog again. "I don't want to get bit."

"That won't be a problem as long as you don't hurt me."

Bolton hated teenagers, but anything felt better than being closed up in the technology center with Dagny. That woman was too much. It had taken him an hour to finally get away from her that one day. He knew nothing about two-way radios or anything electrical for that matter. Charlie stood and nosed closer to his leg.

"How about we start with something easy and we'll work our way up to the blood work." He put the syringe down and instead had her stand on the scale. He recorded her weight and height. Charlie sat obediently beside her. Bolton could just imagine the dog hair silently falling to the floor every time she moved. He checked Mandy's blood pressure, her lungs and finally, her oxygen levels. With nothing else left, he prepared to draw her blood again.

"Okay, here's what we're going to do. You look away and I'll be as careful as I can. Do not jump or scream or cry or anything else. Do we have an agreement?"

Mandy nodded. Charlie scooted closer and touched Bolton's thigh. He jerked back.

"Are you sure this is a good idea?" Mandy asked.

Bolton glared. He wouldn't let the dog, or girl get the upper hand. No way. He picked up the syringe. Charlie's hackles rose, but she moved away from them and toward the door. Bolton used that moment to stick the needle.

"Ouch," Mandy whispered.

The lights went out.

She jerked. Charlie barked.

118

"Don't move," he shouted.

"It's poking. It hurts," Mandy whined.

"Okay, I'm taking it out. Don't do anything." Bolton pulled the needle out and set it on a tray. "Okay, much better. Hold your hand over the area and press hard. That will stop any bleeding." He rose and bumped into the dog. He resisted the urge to brush away the hair he knew had accumulated on his pants. "Move," he barked.

Charlie bumped into him again.

"Don't yell at her," Mandy snapped. "Come here Charlie."

Bolton walked across the pitch-black room, bumping into first a counter, then the bike generator and finally a table before he made it to the wall where he'd hung a penlight. The small beam did little to help the situation. He pointed it at Mandy and the dog. Mandy had her arms around the dog's neck. The two of them sat on the floor.

"Over there is a lamp," he told her. "See it?" He flashed the beam of light on a small desk lamp. "Bring it over." He kept the beam on the lamp as he made his way to the bike. Bolton climbed on and started to pedal.

Mandy unplugged the lamp and turned. "Okay, now bring it over here and plug it in." When Mandy reached his side, he handed her the flashlight.

She fumbled, but finally got the lamp plugged into the bike generator and turned on. "There," she said. The lamp didn't do much for the room, casting only a thin light. "I guess it's better than nothing."

Bolton's thoughts raced. The Biosphere's generators were powered by wind. Phillip had reported the wind had become stronger after the eruption. "What's going on?" Bolton demanded. "How could we lose power?"

Mandy shivered next to him. "Could it be a fire?"

His eyes narrowed. "God, I hope not."

"What about the others?" Mandy asked.

"What about them?" Bolton snapped.

"Should we go and find them?" Charlie still sat facing the door.

"Why do you think your dog barked? What would've made her do that?" he asked.

Mandy shook her head. "I don't know."

"Maybe Phillip turned off the power because he spotted something."

They both turned toward the door.

"We should go find the others," Mandy said.

"We should stay right here," Bolton countered. "They'll eventually come and seek us out. I've the only power source. It won't take long for them to figure that out."

Mandy sat on the floor. Charlie climbed into her lap and almost pushed her over. Bolton kept pedaling.

"How long can you go?" she asked him.

"Miles," he said.

"So how many miles have you gone?"

He glared.

"Are you getting tired?"

"Are you offering to peddle?" He laughed.

Mandy shook her head.

Silence descended and was only interrupted by Charlie's snorts. "Does that dog sleep with you?" he asked.

"Of course!"

"How do you get any rest?"

They were quiet for a few moments, each lost to their own thoughts.

"They aren't coming, are they?" Mandy finally said.

Bolton had begun to worry over that as well. He didn't think it would take long for everyone to figure out where to regroup. Or better yet, for Phillip to fix the generator and get the lights back on.

"Maybe no one else has a flashlight and they're waiting for someone to come to them," Mandy said.

Bolton had to admit the girl could be right.

"We should go and find Francine."

"I should stay here and keep pedaling." He took a deep breath. "Are you okay to wander about by yourself?"

Mandy bit her lower lip. "Sure," she said.

He was unconvinced of her confidence. "You have that brute of a dog. Nothing will surprise her. You'll be fine."

Mandy nodded. "I guess."

"Take the flashlight. But be careful, I don't know how long it will last."

Mandy's eyes became wider.

"Go! Hurry!" he urged.

Mandy rose. She took the flashlight and, with a hand on Charlie, they moved toward the door. "I'll be back with the others soon," she told him.

The beam of light quickly retreated. Bolton had no idea what they would do if they lost power permanently. For sure it would mean they'd have to leave the Biosphere and be forced to wander the harsh landscape, looking for food and shelter. He hit the handlebar with an open palm and then flinched when it stung. They would all die.

* * *

Mandy entered the medical center with Aspen and Charlie right behind her. Aspen had been the final person she'd helped. She fought to keep herself together. Between the people walking overhead and the threats of alien attacks, Mandy felt on edge.

She looked around. Tense faces stared back at her. She always felt like she showed up late and missed all the important information. Mandy leaned toward Evan. She wanted to ask him what had been decided when Francine broke the silence.

"All right. The power is out because the generator has stopped."

Dagny sighed and moved closer to Doc, who still pedaled the bike and produced enough energy for their small lamp.

"Well, where's Phillip? Why isn't he back already? Did he have an idea of why it's failed?" Doc began hammering Francine with questions.

Mandy looked around. She thought she'd seen Phillip headed this way earlier with Francine. She wondered how long the doctor had been badgering her. Doc insisted on a leader and then, every step of the way, he questioned Francine's decisions.

"This is crap. I'm not going to sit here like an idiot, waiting." He jumped off the bike, grabbed a flashlight from the table, and stormed off.

Quickly Evan jumped on the bike, as the light turned off.

"What about our food supply?" Dagny's eyes shifted nervously as she chewed on something.

"The food will be fine," Francine told her. "We need to calm down and wait for Phillip to come back. I'm sure he can fix whatever is wrong.

"Ah need to check the chickens," Aspen said. "Ah just got them eatin' again." She reached for the last remaining flashlight. Before she lifted it off the table, Dagny covered Aspen's hand.

"No, you're not."

Aspen tried to step back. Dagny didn't appear to loosen her grip.

"You're not going to leave us alone," Dagny said.

Mandy thought she sounded close to hysteria.

"Fine, come with me then," Aspen said.

"The animals smell. Besides, they'll all be freaked out."

122

"Well, what do y'all suggest then?" Aspen asked. She pulled her shoulders back. Mandy could see Dagny wouldn't win easily. Aspen stood ready for a fight.

Francine cleared her throat. "Ladies, I think it's important we stick together in this situation. We don't know what Phillip's going to find. But he might need help. We need to stay in one place. Then we can decide what to do next.

"Francine, I have to check on the animals. They could injure themselves if they get frightened. We wouldn't want them to be hurt or die."

Dagny let go of the flashlight and stepped away from Aspen.

"You're right," Dagny said. "Of course. You should check on them.

"Wonderful." Aspen turned on her heel.

"I'll come with you." Evan rose and stepped beside her. Mandy was surprised he sounded so sure of himself.

Dagny mumbled something.

"You all right, Dagny?" Mandy asked.

"Peachy. Great. I almost had the short wave radio working. I almost had an outside human social network. Now, I've got darkness. I've got possible starvation."

"We'll stay here and wait for Bolton and Phillip," Francine said to Mandy, "You go along."

Charlie whined as Aspen, Evan and Mandy walked down the dark hallway.

Everything looked bigger in the darkness of the flashlight. Shadows jumped at them and Mandy quickly became creeped out. She placed her hand on Charlie's head for comfort.

Aspen stopped suddenly and they bumped into each other.

"You okay?" Evan asked.

"Yeah, sure. Thought I saw something move." Mandy heard her take a deep breath. "All right, then," Aspen said and moved forward.

Evan followed with Mandy scurrying to keep up.

Soon Mandy and Aspen sat in a small half circle in the animal bay, while Evan lay with his legs stretched in front of him. Aspen, cross-legged, held one of the smaller chickens in her lap. She rubbed its head and softly hummed to it. Other chickens hovered. Without power there wasn't much they could do except keep the chickens tranquil. The birds were loud right now, but they seemed to be getting calmer than when the group first arrived. Mandy could feel Evan's body heat next to her. His breathing became even and Mandy thought for a moment he'd fallen asleep.

"What will you do if power isn't restored?" Evan asked.

Mandy turned toward him. A blind panic took over and made it difficult for her to get air. "What do you mean?"

"We can't stay here. The plants will die producing CO_2. You'd fall asleep one night and never wake up. Plus the animals wouldn't have food and eventually they'd die as well. No power, means no water. You can only live three days without water. Our precious home will turn on us and become a coffin instead of a haven."

"Yeah, Mandy," Aspen said, "there's no way ah'm stayin' here. No power, walkin' around in the dark, cold, no food and ah'd have to watch my animals die. I'll head for the city instead."

"The city?" Mandy asked confused. "Why would someone want to live in a city where there'd be more people looking for food and shelter."

"Well, to be exact the city of Avondale, Arizona. They built it on top of an entire city that is now underground. I could boil water, stay out of the ash, and have a fire in a trash barrel where the wind wouldn't blow it out."

"How far away is Avondale?"

Aspen shrugged. "A few hours," she hesitated, "by car."

Mandy had a difficult time imagining pretty Aspen with her fancy-dangly earrings walking for days to live in a sewer. Personally Mandy liked above ground living with the ability to take a shower, but who was she to judge.

"I'm takin' my chickens and we'll be on our way."

Mandy shuddered. "I don't want to leave. We don't know where those people on the roof came from or where they're going. I wouldn't want to run into anyone out there. Besides, I like living here with the trees."

"I don't know where those people were headed, but it wasn't towards Avondale. And remember, no power, no trees," Aspen said.

"Evan?" Mandy asked. "What about you?"

"I doubt those people knew where to go. They're probably trying to find the same thing everyone else out there is. Food, shelter, warmth and safety. Maybe they're heading north. I think there are some military bunkers that way. Or East. New York. Maybe New York is good."

"I really don't want to leave and live with rats," Mandy said.

Evan looked at her. His breathing seemed to have returned to the deep even level from before. He closed his eyes. "Well, at least we'd have food," he said chuckling.

Bile rose in Mandy's throat and she gagged. She swallowed hard and fixated on her hands, hoping to stop vomit from rushing into her mouth. Tears streamed down her cheeks. Derek wouldn't find her in the bottom of a rat infested dirty sewer. She was so on edge, every noise startled her.

Chapter 18

∞

Momur entered the staging area and waited. Bodha sighed. His friend had been less than excited over his decision to stay on Terrat to assist the Hu-Mans.

∞-The Hu-Mans have been divided and seem to be working together instead of against one another.-∞

∞-Have they learned to sustain themselves?-∞

Momur blinked. ∞-As well as can be expected. Our Beings have assisted them each in finding shelter.-∞

Bodha looked out over the planet floor and saw how the Hu-Mans closest to the transportation disc lived now in formations created from molded dust. He knew those who were located across the fluid source and up against the peaked planet risings probably resided in rock homes. He wondered if any had been forced to live in the high foliage.

∞-They have also led groups to forage for sustenance. And they've been taught to nurture the Hipiti and harvest it for themselves,-∞ Momur continued.

Bodha could still sense his friend's discomfort. He only answered the questions asked and gave no additional counsel. He hoped soon this whole challenge would be behind them and they could once again be content on Yon-Ya.

∞-They can now take fluid?-∞

Momur nodded.

Learning to submerge their bodies to quench their thirst had been a difficult lesson for those whom he had watched. Bodha hung his head. ∞-Please my friend,-∞ he begged.

∞-Some of the Hu-Mans have seditious ideas.-∞

126

Bodha was startled. He had not sensed these thoughts, but there were so many and even public thoughts had to be attuned one at a time. ∞-Why? We have saved them. Have brought them to a new home and helped them to establish.-∞

∞-We have taken them from their families into the unknown. They are frightened. They think of an uprising. So far, they have taken no action. Have not spoken any verbal commands.-∞

∞-You have attempted to calm them?-∞

Momur nodded. ∞-Yes, but their beings are underdeveloped. I have increased our patrol and have cautioned them to listen well.-∞ Momur's voice lowered. ∞-It is time we return to Yon-Ya. Even now we may find we have stayed away from our planet too long. It may no longer exist. In fact, you may no longer be the Most High Elected.-∞

Bodha gasped. ∞-Why would you declare such?-∞

Momur's voice grew even quieter. ∞-With our planet's communication gone, who knows what has occurred. They are quiet. Perhaps they believe we are lost.-∞

Bodha swirled around the console room. The implications were serious. ∞-It is most unsettling.-∞ Bodha turned to his friend. ∞-We would feel if our planet's peace has been undone. We would know.-∞

Momur drew closer. ∞-You must agree something is occurring. We must leave at once. Must connect with our Beings. We must go home.-∞

Bodha drew his head high. ∞-Prepare at once,-∞ he declared.

Chapter 19

Phillip stood in the lung. He pulled the jacket hood tight, adjusted the facemask, and slid his rough hands into work gloves. Not that long ago he been prepared to only work a few more years before retiring somewhere in the mountains. All that had occurred before the Yellowstone incident. Now there would be no retirement, not for anyone. The best to be wished for was life. Phillip sighed, planted his feet and pulled open the heavy doors. He headed out to fix their electricity problem.

A windstorm whipped ash around, making it impossible to see. He'd need to be able to find his way. Phillip knew the path to the wind generators well, but with the ash it would be easy for someone to become disoriented and lost.

He rounded the corner of the East Lung, the last remaining building that protected him. He didn't want to run into any of the people he'd seen before on the roof. He'd have a hard time explaining how he'd survived with no food, a canteen, a shovel and a flashlight. Even though at every opportunity Mandy proclaimed they might be aliens, Phillip believed they were people in search of safety. Conflicting emotions filled him. They had a roof and warmth. They had food for the time being and even the air seemed fine. It bothered him they had agreed to not let others in. He knew that was wise, but still his heart ached for those lost and wandering.

He wanted to enter the power-box, reset the turbines and return to the Biosphere quickly. He turned the flashlight on. The light, reflected off the ash, and blinded him. Whiteout conditions, he thought. He shook his head. Turning, he went back to the main building. He would need help getting to the turbines.

Phillip entered the Biosphere and removed his clothing and mask carefully. He slipped out of the lung and headed to find the others. He didn't know for sure who would be the best to help. He knew Mandy would volunteer, but didn't know if she had the strength required, or if it would be worth everyone else having to listen to Charlie whine for hours while they were gone. Phillip knew Evan had rock climbed with his father. He would be a good choice. Dagny never went far from her chocolate stash and had seemed quite afraid of heights. He believed Aspen could help, but thought she would be too much of a distraction to Evan. Phillip didn't want anyone getting hurt out there. "Nope, better stick with the guys." He sighed.

"Evan, I need your help," Phillip said as he entered the animal pen a few minutes later.

"Sure, what for?"

"What's wrong with the windmills?" Mandy asked.

"Didn't make it to them. We'll need Bolton too. Then I'll explain." Phillip turned and left, not waiting to see if Evan actually followed. Mandy looked at Aspen who promptly trailed after Evan with the flashlight. Darkness quickly descended and Mandy rushed to keep up with the light. Charlie followed closely behind.

* * *

Phillip entered the medical center. Dagny rode the bike, but little light seemed to be coming from the lamp.

"Bolton, come on," Phillip said. "We need your help."

"With what?" Bolton asked.

"There's too much ash blowing right now. I can't get to the power station alone. And once there we'll probably need to check the turbines anyway. I need a three-man team."

Bolton looked Evan up and down. "Okay, sure. Sounds like fun."

"There are six towers. I can't climb them and we'll most likely need to change the direction of their noses to catch the wind. The ash is blowing hard. We won't be able to see where we're going once we leave the Biosphere."

"We should rope up, tether ourselves to something, so we can find our way back," Evan said.

"I'll get the ropes we used to fix the roof." Phillip left while Bolton and Evan went to find the appropriate clothing for an outside excursion.

"How long are you going to be gone?" Mandy asked not long after, as Phillip struggled to tie a rope around his waist. They stood in the lung.

"Don't know. Usually the maintenance is an all-day project. Maybe six hours or so if we reposition the noses without any problem."

Mandy handed him three food bars. "Francine wanted you to have something in case."

He put them in his pocket before he picked up his canteen. He'd given Evan and Bolton the only two gas masks they had. He didn't like wearing them anyway. Instead he wore two handkerchiefs doubled up over his nose and mouth and safety glasses from the medical center.

"Tell her thanks." Phillip turned and disappeared out the door. Outside, he wondered what Bolton thought about him going outside all the time now. If he hadn't been keeping the ash away, it would have been a challenge even opening the door.

Phillip shuffled toward the six turbines that sat high on the hill. It unnerved him a little having to hike up the towering giants.

For years, when a maintenance problem occurred, they'd called a professional crew. Generally it took six guys, taking turns climbing to fix the multiple problems. Phillip hadn't been

130

sure he believed all of the hype about the turbines. All in all, the old wind generators required about forty hours a year of routine maintenance. It seemed like a lot of work for what they had received in electricity.

Then the Biosphere started to have financial trouble. Some talked of it closing down. One day, not long after, they learned of a government grant, Phillip was whisked away to learn maintenance procedures on some new Mars turbines. Now he felt grateful. Solar power, which is what they'd used before turbines, would have been totally useless to them with the ashen skies, as would have the old turbines.

Phillip carefully placed one foot in front of the other searching for any landmark. While the blowing ash still inhibited visibility, he could now see about six feet in front of him.

Bolton, Evan and Phillip were tied together, Phillip in the lead. He'd located the remaining ropes in the rainforest storage area. They planned to head toward the hill, use landmarks as bases from which they would walk, and keep together so they didn't lose their way.

Phillip's head swiveled back and forth, as he searched for signs of the visitors. There had been great debate on whether to go out or not, but if they didn't start the turbines they would die, so reality won out.

Twenty feet or so from the building, Phillip kicked something. He looked down. Barely sticking out of the ground stood a light. He remembered them to be ten-feet tall and lining the path. Awestruck, Phillip couldn't believe the Yellowstone volcano had released that much ash into the atmosphere. He continued to make his way by sliding his feet forward until he kicked another light. He shook his head.

Excitedly he tugged the rope. The doctor and Evan came rushing through the ash.

"What's going on?" Evan asked.

"Look." Phillip pointed.

131

"Um, okay. That's a light fixture. Good job, "Bolton said sarcastically. "Let's keep moving."

"Yes, we're on the right path. These will lead us up the hill."

Evan nodded and Phillip hurried ahead, sliding one foot in front of the other in search of the next fixture. They moved faster now and before long they reached the base of the turbines.

"How are we going to get in?" Bolton asked.

"I have the keys."

Phillip carefully climbed the bottom stair. Each turbine had a short metal stairwell that led to doors that opened inward. A thin film of ash had settled on the framework. Glad of the holes in the metal, he noticed most of the ash had drifted down and past the steps. The staircase swayed to the left. Phillip stopped and waited for the shifting to subside. He took another step and a gust of wind blew the stairwell, causing it to lean further. Phillip lost his grip on the railing. He tumbled over the side. As soon as he hit the ground, a bar holding the stair to the turbine broke off, flying through the air and out into the vast expanse of ash cloud.

Evan rushed to him. "You okay?"

Phillip struggled to breathe. He stood, wobbly at first. Evan steadied him. Bolton stood a distance away.

"I'm all right. Let's try the next turbine." Phillip, Evan and Bolton headed toward the second one.

Once again Phillip ascended the metal stairwell. He shifted his weight evenly as he climbed. Gripping the railing, his knuckles turned white. He made it to the top, fished out the key and attempted to stick it in the lock. Nothing, he shoved harder, but the key stopped.

Chapter 20

∞

Dahi shifted with excitement on his pillows. Rohongra's discs were close. He could feel the ThAak-Toons energy. When they landed Dahi could finally take his place as Most High. The doors opened and ThAak-Toons floated toward him.

∞-Where's Rohongra hiding her thoughts?-∞ Dahi's Being was filled with glee.

∞-We have left her to the fate of Yon-Ya, Most Supreme,-∞ thought one of the Beings.

∞-How could you be so stupid. She could gain their trust. Find the power to attack us.-∞

∞-Most Supreme, we brought you the Hu-Mans.-∞ The nameless ThAak-Toon bowed to Dahi. ∞-Our holds are full.-∞

∞-Well unload them at once,-∞ Ka thought as he drew near. Dahi saw his lips turn up.

Dahi shuddered as the intense feeling entered his Being. Ka taking control of his Hu-Mans overwhelmed him, but he did not want to anger Ka. He needed to be closer to achieving his goal before he made his move.

∞-You heard Most High Ka's thought transfers. Unload the Hu-Mans over to the pens.-∞

Dahi moved his Being towards Ka, his lips slightly turned upright. Dahi began to feel at peace. Maybe now he could begin his plan to rid Rohongra of her life force. Ka moved away from the group. Dahi felt unsure of Ka's thoughts, closed now to him, but guessed the Most High felt pleased with this discovery of extra Hu-Mans.

∞-Before you leave, Most High, where shall the remaining ThAak-Toons reside?-∞

∞-No matter to me.-∞ Ka waved a dismissive limb.

∞-May we reside among your Beings?-∞

∞-For now.-∞

Dahi instructed his Beings to move among Celute's. His thoughts were quiet to most. He let only a select few be privy to the thoughts of harm he vowed for Rohongra's Being.

* * *

Rohongra lay on the Roeds blossoms. The planets had risen around them and dotted the heavens above. The Hu-Mans had settled down to their rest before the last large bodies entered the skyline. She saw the ochre planet, Celute, and it's sienna colored moon and verdant smaller moon body. Farther away she made out the flame-colored planet of TE-Garon and its five moons all shimmering masses of ash.

After the Hu-Man had connected with her thoughts, Rohongra became wary. She kept across the camp and away from him studying his actions for a possible threat. She had seen how he gravitated toward two younger beings and assisted them kindly. He wiped their faces gently and lifted his lips. She had even heard a burbling sound issue forth. She sensed he comforted them. Still she was nervous and unsure what to think of a Hu-Man who could hear her thoughts.

Rohongra rose and swiftly crossed to the area where the Hu-Man slept with the two younger beings. They huddled together, drawn to each other's warmth, their limbs tangled as the furry Padwi did when they were first born, all burrowing close together.

They looked as if they could cause no harm. Rohongra blinked. She wondered if the Hu-Man could hear all her Beings' thoughts and if so, what else had he heard?

Thought transfer was done one Being to one Being. Public thoughts were easily read by any who wished to focus on an individual. And then the private thoughts were just that, private to one. When sending thought transfers, it became possible to select a Being and send a private thought to only them. Her thoughts, when she had communicated with the Hu-Man, had been private between them. Now she also wondered if those on her planet had been wrong. Could the Hu-Mans communicate using thought transfer without touch? How would this impact her? Her Beings? The concept stopped her. Did she even have any Beings left? Those who survived the blast might be swayed by Dahi's lies or Ka's strength.

She wondered what it meant that she had not heard from Dahi. She shuddered. Rohongra knew she could always open thought communication with him, but for some reason, the idea brought intense feelings to her Being. She sensed danger. Did it come from the Hu-Man or from Dahi? Or did it come from Yon-Ya? She hoped they wouldn't act until Most High Bodha returned. She felt confident she could reason with him.

Rohongra turned from her study of the Hu-Mans and saw the great fluid source had peaked. Carefully she made her way closer. The organisms that called the source home shown iridescent and lit the surface of the pool. As she watched they drew closer to each other becoming blushed. They lifted up, dancing on the surface and pooling higher and higher, reaching toward the sky. Gingerly she lifted her limb and caressed the bodies closest to her. The fluid wrapped around her limb and tickled as it slid first up and then down. Suddenly the organisms pulled away and floated before her.

∞-I did not mean to startle them.-∞

The Hu-Man stood behind her. She was weakened from the realization she hadn't heard him nor felt his presence.

She steadied herself and calmly thought. ∞-They are Cifoli. They live in the pool and only come to the surface when the sky is darkened.-∞

∞-They are beautiful. I have never seen anything like this.-∞ The Hu-Man burbled forth noise and the Cifoli reared back. ∞-Oh, no. I do not mean to frighten them. I just realized I have never seen anything like anything on this planet. Kind of silly.-∞

Rohongra reached for the Hu-Man's limb and clasped it. Lifting their limbs together, she held them out to the Cifoli. Her thoughts surged forward. ∞-We mean no harm.-∞

The Cifoli merged, waved and then finally wrapped around both their limbs.

The Hu-Man gasped. ∞-What a rush!-∞ he thought.

Chapter 21

Evan gripped the wheel again. His muscles bulged under his shirt as he attempted to turn the nose of the third turbine into the wind.

The first two they had found had broken blades. In order to know that though, you had to climb all the way to the top because of the limited visibility. Getting in had also been a challenge. They used the shovel to break the covering of ash so the key would fit in the lock.

The climb up the four flights of stairs was exhausting despite the fact he had regularly rock climbed for years. Weeks in the dome had made him lazy and out of shape. He'd have to keep climbing the trees in the rainforest. He used his shirt to wipe sweat from his brow and the palms of his hands.

He gazed out of the round plastic tube he sat in. Ash blew, blocking him from seeing the dome. Evan closed his eyes and conjured up the images of the scenery he saw the last time he climbed with his dad. They'd talked about it for years. The Tetons. His father organized every minute of the trip and on graduation had surprised Evan with the new gear they would need.

A weeklong excursion. They saw Yellowstone Park, Jackson Hole and finished up at the top of the Tetons overlooking the great valley below. Despite all the research and books, Evan had never seen anything as beautiful as the peaks of the Tetons and the world that lay quietly around them.

Evan wiggled, pulled his wallet out of his back pocket and looked at the photo he kept close. Another member of their climbing party took it for them. His dad stood tall next to him, a proud smile on his face and his arm casually draped around Evan. Tears sprang up and he quickly wiped them away. The view behind them rose in beautiful splendor, while his current dark and scary landscape produced a lot of unknowns.

Sighing he turned back to the job in front of him. They would wonder down below what took him so long. Phillip had been considered part of the ground crew and the knowledge he shared about the turbines, was the equivalent to Evan reading it in a book, and as accurate. Phillip informed Evan he would need to put oil in the big machine in the middle. However, that "big machine" wasn't "big" and the oil went in a little tube, not clearly marked, causing Evan several minutes of uncertainty. It took Evan another fifteen minutes to locate the funnel that helped get oil into the tiny round tube. Then Evan climbed into the white hollow egg-looking thing in the middle of the turbine. He squeezed his frame into the hole. Locating the wheel had been the easy part. Actually turning the nose into the wind, though, challenged him. Evan struggled to move it half an inch. He had to catch the wind exactly.

Evan squirmed to get a different grip on the wheel. No way would he climb back down and ask Doc for help. Neither did he plan to leave the dome and move into the sewers. He placed his hands evenly on the wheel and gripped it, tugging hard. It gave a little. He stopped and caught his breath. He gave one more good hard tug.

Something clicked. The nose finally appeared to be in position. "Done," he called down not sure if they could hear him. He crawled backwards out of the egg and onto the first set of stairs. Evan hooked his carabineer to the stair rail. Four flights of stairs in each turbine needed to be navigated, along with three platforms at various levels. He slowly descended, stopping at level two for a quick drink and then continued. Evan's throat felt parched but he kept reminding himself to conserve his water. He reached the last stair and jumped down.

"You all right? You're sweating a lot," Doc asked.

"I'm fine, but it's hard work. When you get up to the top you have to climb on the outside of the railing to squeeze through the nose. Once in the egg, you access it sideways. Took me a couple of tries to loosen the wheel enough to move it."

Doc nodded, zipped up his coat, put his gas mask back on and pulled his gloves up as far as they would go.

"How long did I take?" Evan asked Phillip. He felt sure it was a record-breaking time of thirty minutes.

Phillip chuckled. "Almost two hours. Good for a rookie. Just think, one down, three more to go."

Evan and Phillip placed their facemasks on. Phillip gave an all clear to Doc and pulled open the door. Ash quickly swirled around their feet. They tied up and made their way down the stairs and to the next turbine. No reason to risk someone getting lost out there.

Two hours? This would take all day, Evan thought. He became determined to be faster on the next one. He already imagined his hero's return.

* * *

Phillip heard the echoing footsteps as Evan descended the stairs in the last turbine. He looked at his watch for the hundredth time. They were almost done. Bolton had taken one. The blade had been broken in another, which would leave them with half the power. That was, of course, if this one stayed intact. Phillip believed with some creativity he could keep the Biosphere in balance with just the three.

The kid had done great. After five hours of trudging in the ash, Evan took his turn again on the last turbine. This let

Bolton rest at the bottom. Phillip's stomach growled. He caught a dirty look from Bolton, ignored him and paced.

"Again, I sure hope you're right about the wind direction, Phillip. I'm exhausted and I don't want to do this again anytime soon."

Phillip nodded in agreement. He saw Evan as he swung onto the platform between the second and third stairwell.

"So, what does it mean to us if we only have half the power? How much trouble will we be in?"

"We'll get started with what we have. Figure out the rest later," Phillip said.

"What the hell does that mean?" A thud accompanied by a sickening scream pierced the air and interrupted them. Phillip grabbed the bottom rail and began to climb. He felt Bolton's hand on his arm.

"I'll go."

"Hurry."

Evan's screams echoed off the metal walls. Phillip was thankful for the noise. It meant Evan still lived. For now anyway. He didn't want to lose the kid.

Phillip saw Bolton had already reached him. "What's going on?" Phillip yelled.

"He fell. I need to reset his knee. He's banged up. When I'm done we need to get him down from here."

Phillip heard Evan, but couldn't make out any of the words. He watched helplessly as Evan gripped the rail. His scream echoed. He should have at least attempted to climb one. The kid had probably tired. Phillip shook his head as he watched.

"Okay, his knee is back in place," Bolton had leaned over the railing and called down to him.

"That's all? His knee?" Phillip asked.

"Well, I can't tell if there's internal bleeding obviously, but everything seems okay. Evan thinks he can climb down. I'm going to help him in case he slips again."

140

"Shouldn't we lower him?"

"That would take too long. He'll hop." Evan hung onto the stairwell. His arms gripped the rails while one leg steadied him on the stair and the other dangled. Bolton descended behind him.

Another thud and scream filled the hollow tube they were confined by.

"He's okay. Banged his knee against the rail," Bolton yelled.

Phillip began to pace. He felt useless in his old man's body. He should've been the one up there, not Evan. After all, he had gone out with the crew every time these things needed maintenance. But Phillip had always been at the bottom, a tired old man, stuck at the lower rail of life.

Evan and Bolton finally reached him, pulling Phillip from his thoughts.

"You okay?" Phillip asked.

"Yeah," Evan said between clenched teeth. They set him down on the floor with his back against the wall.

"I'm going to head to the power station and see if I can re-route everything. Stay here," Phillip instructed.

"We should rope up. It'd be easy for you to lose your bearings and get lost," Bolton said.

"I'll be fine. The power house is nearby."

"I've been in storms like this before. It's disorienting. A friend of mine went off the road once. He left the car and never returned. They found him only ten feet away. I'm sure he had no idea how close the vehicle sat. Instead he . . ." Bolton shook his head.

Phillip took the rope from Bolton's out-stretched hand.

Bolton nodded. "Be careful," he said.

Phillip turned and left. He needed to redeem himself by completing this task and getting the kid back to the Biosphere safe and sound. Almost there, he thought. One foot in front of the other. He stopped when he finally reached the power center. He said a quick prayer. If he wasn't able to flip a power switch and get it all working now . . . he shook his head, and took out his key. Phillip stuck it in the door. An invisible force stopped it. He took off his glove and tried to turn the key again. It didn't budge. Ash must have accumulated inside this lock. He shoved the key one more time and turned it hard. Afraid to break it off in the lock, he removed it, but then quickly realized it probably didn't matter anyway.

Think, he told himself. There had to be an option. Phillip stood back, arms crossed and waited for the perfect idea that would gain him access. Without power they'd die. He had no choice. He took his shovel and held it high above his head. Taking a step back, he hit the lock several times, finally breaking the wooden doorjamb.

Once inside he gave a sigh of relief. He shut the door, took off his mask, and removed his goggles. The darkness enveloped him. He took his flashlight from his pocket and flipped it on. It wasn't a big help, but better than nothing. He moved towards the left corner of the room. Control levers with big black bulbs waited for him. Phillip turned the knobs, flipped a switch, and pushed the three levers for the remaining turbines. A green light blinked on and he heard a quiet whirr from below. A smile spread across his face.

"We have power," Phillip sang out, buttoning his coat and turning to leave.

Something small and black caught his eye. How did a kitten find its way in there? He poked it with his boot. Quickly realizing his mistake, he gasped and began to cough as dust drifted in the air toward him. A shudder ran down the length of his body. He turned and fled, tying himself to the rope as he ran.

Chapter 22

∞

∞-Most High, your council chambers are prepared and all Beings you have requested are present.-∞ Soluma-Rah's second-in-command, Gramar nodded.

Soluma-Rah heard his thoughts but did not move toward her chamber. She needed a moment to calm her Being. Her eyes shuttered, blocking the light, and she focused on her limbs. Moments passed and she felt most ready to begin her thought transfer to her planet.

∞-As you are all aware, ThAak-Toons have been evaporated. The loss of life force is determined to be great. Most High Rohongra currently awaits the Most High Bodha to return to Yon-Ya, and Dahi has joined Ka on Celute. I have been made aware some Hu-Mans have also been deposited on Yon-Ya, but most have gone to Celute. Thoughts have not been clear if the Most Supreme Dahi has brought them to Ka or if he is still negotiating for his own Being. I come to you for a decision. Collective action must be taken to save and protect our Beings.-∞

∞-Most High, do you believe such force is necessary? Will we not be provoking Ka?-∞ a council member shared thought.

∞-If Ka gains numbers and attacks our planet, we will not find safety. Ka wishes for supreme power. He pursued this desire during the first war.-∞ It had at first seemed clear Ka would never slow his terror long enough for peace to be found. Now would he continue to attack until all other Beings' life force had drained?

∞-If he has access to Hu-Mans, who could be trained to fight for him, it may give Ka the ability to overpower once more.-∞

∞-Most High, what is your plan now that Duji is no more?-∞ another council member inquired.

∞-One conflict at a time. We must first ready for affray. Our Beings must increase their physical exertion. When affray first began, many were no older than a few moons. We are only aware of the agony because of our elder's epic tales. We must teach all our Beings the power of Ten-Dati and also re-initiate the stories of our dark past.-∞

∞-What version of the war shall we tell, Most High?-∞

∞-Our rising at morning's awakening was to rays of hot fotia falling around us. Our Beings' skin bubbled and oozed. Cries of agony rang among the young and older Beings who could not enter the caves. Many life forces ceased. Talk of our Beings lying flat and suffering. Use images that will draw our Beings to move as one.-∞

The council Beings conferred. Soluma-Rah let their thoughts have reign.

∞-Most High, they are not prepared for this. We have so few of the right ekton. Up against the power of Celute, our life forces will perish quickly.-∞ The Being seemed unsure to stand before her.

∞-Let us train the Hu-Mans to aid us,-∞ another's thoughts broke in.

∞-What?-∞

∞-If Ka can use and train his Hu-Mans to help his cause. Why not train ours?-∞

Soluma-Rah closed her thoughts for a moment. Her body filled with pain at the possibility of losing so many Beings to war.

∞-Most High, it is the only way. Your thoughts have to align that way as well,-∞ Gramar thought.

144

∞-Should their life force be traded for our cause and other's selfish choices?-∞ a council member joined in.

∞-War is war. There will be no protection for them. When Ka attacks and rains destruction down around us, they will only be left helpless. This has become a new home for the Hu-Mans. Without it they will be no better off than if they'd stayed on their own planet.-∞

∞-You think truth. Go with haste. Communicate this need to the Hu-Mans. Let them know the great risk we all face when war comes, so they are in line with our path. I caution you, the Hu-Mans must learn the danger Ka may bring, but we must be careful they do not choose to rebel once they gain this knowledge. Show them first and then hopefully they will fight with us willingly, not against us.-∞

∞-Most High, what age?-∞ her second asked.

Soluma-Rah's Being filled with confusion. ∞-What age?-∞

∞-What age of Hu-Mans shall we train?-∞

∞-Their age of twelve or higher.-∞

∞-Their bodies will most benefit us.-∞

Chapter 23

Mandy paced back and forth in the medical center and fiddled with the flashlight. Aspen sat with her feet on the desk and Dagny snored in the corner on the exam table. Shortly after her last turn on the bike, Dagny had grabbed a blanket and pillow and hadn't moved since. Francine peddled at a slow but steady pace. Mandy felt exhausted but wasn't able to close her eyes, and as time ticked on she could feel herself become more anxious.

"How long do you think they've been gone?" Mandy asked, her voice sounded desperate to her own ears.

"About seven hours. I'm sure they're fine," Francine said.

"But they've been gone longer than expected. What if they're lost or what if they don't come back at all? Then what are we supposed to do? We can't stay here without power." She touched the necklace she wore, gripping her parent's rings.

"Calm down. Phillip is very competent. Again, I'm sure everything is great."

"But they should have been back by now. We should go and find them. Phillip said it's a big job. Maybe, we could help." Her gaze darted toward the door.

"Mandy, even if that were true, we don't have rope. If the ash is as bad as Phillip said, we wouldn't make it."

The lights in the medical center began to flicker. Mandy jumped up and down screeching excitedly. Charlie howled next to her.

"I know girl, we're saved," she told Charlie.

"What the, what's going on?" Dagny asked.

"The power is on," Mandy screamed and rushed out of the room with Francine and Aspen close behind. They raced down the hall and stared through the window into the Savannah. It was pitch black.

Mandy blinked. "Where are the rest of the lights?" she asked, confused.

"I don't know. Maybe, there's a problem with a breaker."

They waited what seemed to be hours, but more likely several minutes.

"Look, flashlights." Francine pointed to a spot below where light peeked through the trees before disappearing again. Mandy turned and ran with Charlie at her feet, eager to find out what was going on now. "What happened?" Francine's question went unanswered.

They moved out to the balcony and watched as Phillip and Bolton supported Evan through the biomes. Mandy could tell Evan had hurt his leg. She noticed he put no pressure on it, but all three men looked shaken.

They followed the three guys all the way to the medical center before Phillip finally reported. "He fell." He and Bolton lifted Evan onto the table.

"Help him lay down," Bolton ordered. He turned away and washed his hands at the sink.

"Fell? From the top of the windmill?" Francine's tone of voice rose higher than normal.

"No, he would've been dead if that had happened." Bolton returned to the table to find them all gathered around. "Please move. I need to examine him."

"Yes, everyone stand back," Dagny said. She used her hands to guide people several steps away. Then she stood at Bolton's side. "Do you need an assistant?" she asked.

Bolton shook his head. "I'm good," he said.

Dagny held her ground.

"How badly is he hurt?" Francine wanted to know.

Bolton looked her in the eye and didn't answer.

"I have a sinking feeling in my stomach," Dagny said. She looked down at Evan. He lay creepily still. His eyes were closed and his breathing slower.

"He's going to die?" Dagny whispered.

Evan's eyes opened wide and he struggled to sit.

"No, he's not," Bolton assured. "Kid, it's all right." He patted Evan's shoulder and pushed him back while he gave Dagny a withering look. "He took a good fall."

"Twenty feet," Phillip added.

"And dislocated his knee. I put it back in place right away, but there's some swelling. I'm going to wrap it. And I want to check for any internal injuries. If you could leave us . . ." Bolton grabbed his stethoscope.

"But you were able to get power," Mandy said.

"Half power," Phillip told them. He coughed into his sleeve.

"Do you need someone to go out and help with the rest of the windmills?" Francine asked.

"I'm not getting involved with that," Dagny said. "If Evan came back hurt from doing whatever they'd been doing, I'm not even going to try." She stood at Bolton's elbow.

Phillip coughed again. "It wouldn't help. We got all the turbines that could be turned on, into the wind. The others will have to be repaired before we can use them." Phillip sank into a chair.

Dagny caught Bolton watching Phillip.

"So y'all what does that mean?" Aspen wanted to know.

"Phillip says we can survive on half power if we're careful," Bolton said.

"How?" Francine asked.

148

Phillip cleared his throat. "Each part of the dome will get twelve hours of light."

"Will that work?" Aspen asked.

"It'll have to," Bolton said. "Evan, your knee will be fine. I want you to keep it wrapped. I'm not seeing anything else of a concern, but I'm going to keep you here for the night so I can observe you."

"What about food production?" Dagny asked Evan. All the others glared at her. As if in her own defense she turned and spoke, "After all, Bolton said our plant expert has only hurt his knee"

Bolton shook his head.

"The power station and turbine system were built with redundancy in mind. Not to mention, plants are used to day and night. We shouldn't have a problem," Phillip assured them.

"Perhaps we need a backup plan. I mean after all, we can't survive without food," Dagny said.

Bolton stepped on Dagny's foot as he returned to Evan with a blanket and pillow. "Sorry," he huffed. "Perhaps now you could join the group over there so he can rest?"

The way Bolton pointed to the others, Mandy didn't really think it a suggestion. She watched as Dagny finally stepped away.

"Dagny, I think the only backup plan we need is attached to the two-way radio. Why don't you get it working?" Francine said.

"That's a great idea, y'all. We could find out if others have survived and where they all are. Ah mean we don't even know if this is a West Coast problem. The East Coast could be fine. Maybe we just need to get over the Rockies to safety."

Mandy didn't think so, but she liked that it might be possible. She didn't want to talk about all the earthquakes that had happened around the world before the big explosion, or how at the end The President had inferred the human race might not survive. Some people were just negative thinkers. Maybe Aspen was onto something.

"Phillip, I still need your help with the radio. I've played with the wires, but I'm not really sure what I'm doing," Dagny said.

Phillip nodded and struggled to rise.

"You okay?" Doc asked, quickly crossing the room to help him up.

"Sure." Phillip coughed again into his sleeve.

"After you're done, come back and let me check you out. I don't like the sound of that cough. It came on awfully quick."

Phillip grunted and followed Dagny toward the tech room next door.

Chapter 24

∞

∞-All is well?-∞ Bodha thought.

The transportation disc entered the Yon-Ya atmosphere and hovered above the home of their Beings. Bodha felt relief to find the planet whole and undisturbed. His thoughts went out to those below.

The Beings in the disc surrounding him did not respond, but followed his thoughts with an intensity he'd never noticed before. They were all worried. He searched their minds to find the cause.

∞-Momur, return the disc to its place,-∞ Bodha commanded. The ship had roved over their home. Below their Beings watched and waited, moving toward the landing site.

Momur quieted, the other Beings did as well. The disc landed and Bodha swirled through them to be the first to descend onto the planet. The council waited, the rest of the Beings surrounding them.

Bodha nodded.

∞-We are relieved you are well,-∞ the Second of the council thought. ∞-We'd feared for your safety. We received no communication.-∞

It was a rebuke. Bodha sensed Momur behind him. Sensed the unease of the situation. He rose up. ∞-Things needed to be handled.-∞ Bodha made to move away.

∞-Why did you not respond?-∞ Another member of the council dared think.

Bodha's look steeled. He gave no answer.

∞-You left and allowed other Beings to occupy our planet,-∞ the Second concurred but with deference to his station.

∞-You put our life force at risk,-∞ a fourth Being joined in the discussion.

Bodha was taken aback. He had never seen a member of his council, or even his planet, express such anger. Momur stood beside him and Bodha felt gratitude. He knew how Momur felt, yet he portrayed alliance. Bodha's thoughts raged a war inside of him. Finally he bowed. ∞-I accept your emotions.-∞

Slowly the council backed away and acknowledged his status. He searched their minds and found no desire for revolt. ∞-Where are the Hu-Mans?-∞

Momur moved beside him as they made their way to the abodes. Bodha knew he'd have to do something with them, but he wanted no further question regarding his motives. Perhaps the Hu-Mans could reside on the planet without incident for a short time before being relocated, allowing him to regain his position.

Momur followed close by. Still protective. Still mindful of the reception.

∞-It's not just the Hu-Mans who were left to us.-∞

At this news, Bodha stopped. ∞-What?-∞

∞-The Most High Being of ThAak-Too resides with the Hu-Mans in the tors.-∞

No wonder his Beings stirred. Bodha searched their faces, their minds. ∞-ThAak-Toons have sought war?-∞ How had his peaceful Beings isolated the invaders?

∞-It is only the Most High. Her Beings abandoned her,-∞ the Second in council thought. Bodha's eyes searched the ragged hills to which they spoke. ∞-We are well aware it is an act of war. But we had no way to remove her. All the transportation discs . . .-∞

Bodha gestured for them to move on.

∞-We also asked for assistance from TE-Garon, but they have not responded. We have stayed vigilant and have prepared for possible attack.-∞ The thoughts became private. Too many Beings crowded around. How aware they were of the impact of the situation, Bodha was unsure, but he now knew why the council had greeted him with anger. He would not proclaim Rohongra's whereabouts.

∞-What of her other Beings?-∞

∞-They are no more. The only to survive are the ones who had gone with Rohongra to harvest the Hu-Mans. They are the same ones who have left her here. Her second, Dahi has taken shelter on Celute and has gathered all the ThAak-Toons who traveled to the Water Planet to him. We await their return.-∞

Bodha hesitated briefly. ∞-What of Ka?-∞ he asked the Second.

∞-Exactly.-∞

Chapter 25

Mandy gazed across the metal table in the tech center to Francine. Phillip and Dagny sat next to her messing with the wires inside an old box radio-receiver, and Aspen stood over them. They focused on the radio, but Mandy worried about Evan. He'd looked really pale when Doc examined him. Mandy had wanted to stay in the medical center to keep him company, but not with Doc issuing demands. Instead, she was stuck trying to fix items she knew little about and were older than her.

"Francine," Mandy said, getting her attention. "Do you think Evan's going to be okay?"

"I'm sure he'll be fine, dear," she said.

Phillip coughed. Francine scooted her chair out of range. Aspen cleared her throat and looked over to meet Mandy's eyes.

"Ah don't know, ma'am, he looked pretty beat up. Not to mention the job in the agricultural area is physically demanding. Even if he's okay, it's ah goin' to take awhile for him to be able to do his job again," Aspen said.

"Then we'll have to pitch in and help," Francine said.

"Would you shush? I can't hear over all your chitchat. Besides, he'll be fine. Bolton is with him." Dagny adjusted another wire and then began to slowly turn one of the knobs. Phillip attempted to stifle a cough and Dagny shot him a glare.

Francine rose. "I'm going to get some snacks. It seems we're going to be here awhile. And Phillip, that cough sounds nasty. I'll bring back some hot tea for you."

"Great, I'd like some brownies," Dagny said.

154

"I bet you would. I'll grab some fruit instead." Francine stepped toward the door, but stopped when static filled the room. A faint voice broke through the silence of the group. Mandy looked up from her lap. She'd been studying the back of her hands, and was now shocked they had the thing working. It sounded like they had someone on the other end. Everyone except Phillip seemed to scoot closer to hear what the girl said.

"KLZ28V, this is Red station on the West Coast. We are ten survivors and have not seen the sun in forty," there was a cough, "-nine days. We are able to get a decent amount of water purified. Thanks, Rushmore Central for the tip. Food supply is beginning to get low, and we've sent a group out to forage. No new survivors have shown themselves."

"Oh my, there are survivors," Francine said as she simultaneously lifted her hand to cover her mouth.

"We have to respond," Dagny stated. "What should our message be?"

Mandy could feel the excitement in the room growing and the energy in the air instantly changed.

"We need a name," Dagny said. "How about the Biospherians."

"No," Francine snapped, surprising Mandy. "That will give too much away."

"Okay, what about, 'House of Glass'?" Dagny suggested again.

Mandy sat back and observed the group. Phillip coughed and Mandy shifted her gaze to study his face.

"Ah like that," Aspen said.

"It's perfect," Francine exclaimed.

"What else should we tell them?" Dagny asked. "Food supply holding out?"

"Ah don't know. Do y'all really want to tell people that? We don't want to tempt anyone," Aspen said. Dagny's eyes widened.

"I think we should tell them our name and how many people. Leave it at that," Phillip said.

"Okay," Dagny agreed. She picked up the mike and pushed the button ready to give their short message to the world.

* * *

Bolton rushed into the tech room and yanked the radio's microphone from Dagny's, pudgy hand. He recoiled when one of his fingers touched hers. A smile spread across her face. He quickly moved away. "Are you guys crazy? We're in one of the safest places on this planet. Our food is holding out, we have electricity, running water to drink, and lamb if we need meat." He turned toward Aspen as he said that. "All of this is a luxury, and to some would be worth killing for." Someone to his right sighed, but he didn't turn to see whom. "You can be mad or upset all you want, but we have to be rational about this."

"Bolton, our families could be out there somewhere. They might be dying. Suffering the fate of starvation or dehydration and we could save them," Francine said.

"That's a long-shot we can't afford to hope for and you know it. How could you be so naïve, silly and emotional? Millions of people are scattered around the world. And several million more probably didn't survive. The others, well who knows where they are or what fate they're enduring," Bolton said.

He shook his head at the emotional idiocy of the woman. Bolton couldn't believe she called the shots for their group. At this point he believed Mandy would have been a better leader than Francine, he could at least manipulate her.

"Why does it matter if we tell them a generic name and how many people are here?" Dagny questioned.

"Well, what if it's the government or some other group who's tracking people to gather resources for their families?"

156

"Why would they do that?" Mandy asked.

"I don't know, but I don't think all the pieces of our disaster are adding up. Who knows who is truly behind this?"

"He's right," Francine said. "Close your mouth Bolton, it's not that big of a deal. We don't know who these other groups are or how close they are to us. I want a rotation of people monitoring this radio twenty-four seven, taking notes. We need to learn more about them. No out-going pillow talk, Dagny. You understand?"

Dagny mumbled something and Bolton turned to leave. Phillip caught his eye on the way out when he coughed and seemed to have trouble catching his breath. "Phillip get something for that cough would you. You'll keep the animals up all night. I'm sure Francine has some honey or lemon or something. Don't want you infecting anyone. And Francine isn't your only job to keep us eating healthy?"

Bolton didn't wait for an answer. He didn't need one because he'd already won the fight. It was just a matter of time before he'd be in charge. He whistled a tune his mother used to sing to him. A smile played across his lips. Oh yeah, just a matter of time.

Chapter 26

∞

Starlight had risen to the center of the sky. Rohongra stood beneath the Burrows while the Hu-Mans took their meal. Her eyes twitched merrily. The Hu-Mans seemed most adaptable. They acted as though no harm could befall them. Rohongra hoped there was truth in that.

∞-It is a good place,-∞ E'nov thought.

Rohongra had given the Hu-Man who could think, a name, 'One Who Gathers Others.' Even now the youngest of the Hu-Mans stayed close to him.

Rohongra agreed. The Yon-Yas had a much better life. ∞-Much better than ThAak-Too.-∞

∞-That's where you're from? Your planet? ThAak-Too?-∞

Her lower lip trembled and her eyes found the sky.

∞-You miss your home? I understand. I miss Earth. And my parents and friends, oh and cheeseburgers, even though this fruit - these burrows are tasty.-∞

∞-I miss,-∞ Rohongra couldn't continue her thought. What did she have to miss? A hot star that crushed and drained life force? Her father resided in the galaxy from where no one ever comes back. She had lost her mother. She had no one to trust. What did that leave her? Her Being ached. Her head bowed. ∞-My home is no more.-∞

The Hu-Man separated himself from the young ones and moved closer to her. ∞-I heard – I mean . . .-∞

Rohongra sensed the challenge in E'nov's thoughts. He heard, but not in the way he heard the vocalizations of his

158

beings. So what was imaging and what real thought? Those on her planet grew into thought at a very young age, releasing imagining and the ability to pretend. Several of the Hu-Man offspring ran around, playing at some antic. She missed the days of imagining. She had also missed the company of offspring.

∞-My Beings have destroyed the planet of my origin. It no longer exists.-∞

E'nov's brow furrowed. ∞-How can you be sure? Perhaps . . .-∞

Rohongra shook her head. ∞-No perhaps. I felt their demise.-∞ She touched the center of her being. ∞-We know of life-force loss. We feel it.-∞

E'nov touched his center with his appendages. He shook his head.

Frustrated, Rohongra swirled to her feet and returned to the pool. She needed to feel full. She stepped in and let the fluid flow over and into her. Emotions swirled and fought. What should she do? What did Dahi plan? Would he persuade those of her planet and Celute she must be dealt with? She gulped in fluid and it calmed her. Still her thoughts raged. If only she could remain on Yon-Ya. Even remain right here, without the luxury of Polisis or the warmth of Duji. She had no idea how long she had remained submerged, at one with fluid, but when her head broke the surface, she found herself surrounded. Not only by the Hu-Man offspring, but also by the council of Yon-Ya. She twirled in the fluid to get a sense of what was to be.

Her eyes found Most High Bodha and she realized all of her questions would now be answered. She would learn of her fate. Suddenly her center grew fearful. Her breathing quickened. Liquid formed and pooled at the bottom of her eyes. She took a deep breath of fluid and calmed her being before she moved slowly across the pool and toward Most High Bodha. E'nov stood still some distance away, but he followed her movement with his eyes and tried to draw as close as he could. Yon-Yas held the Hu-Mans back. Some of the younger ones, bored by the situation, still played in the fields beyond, oblivious to the solemnity of the moment.

The Yon-Ya leaders backed away from the pool, allowing her to join them on the bank.

∞-Most High Bodha.-∞ Rohongra bowed her head. They were equal in the universe, but not on Yon-Ya. On Yon-Ya she had to be considered a prisoner who could be dealt with in any way they saw fit.

∞-Most High,-∞ Bodha replied.

Rohongra felt a modicum of relief. He referred to her by her elected title. Perhaps he would not be quick to remove her life force. She drew her power in, trying to protect herself and remind all who stood near of what she once had been.

∞-I am most pleased to witness your safe return. It has been many rotations. I am sure all have been concerned.-∞ Her limbs swept over the sea of bodies from Yon-Ya. Their thoughts were all closed to her.

E'nov moved nearer. He stood close to the Most High of Yon-Ya. The other Beings seemed not to notice, but Bodha's eyes found and studied him, a question on his face.

∞-Your Beings have been most kind to have offered asylum,- ∞ Rohongra thought, trying to distract Bodha from E'nov, though why, she was unsure.

∞-You are faring well?-∞

Rohongra nodded, her body warmed by the breeze. E'nov's thoughts followed hers, his eyes strained to see her slightest reaction. She lifted her lips and turned her attention to Bodha.

∞-Most High, have you determined my future?-∞ she inquired.

E'nov's gasp drew astonished glances his way. Quickly he pretended to have stepped on something. The Yon-Yas looked toward their leader. E'nov watched them both.

∞-I have much to convey.-∞ Bodha stepped back. ∞-Come.-∞

Rohongra glided behind Bodha as they exited the tors. She had momentarily thought about asking E'nov to join her, but she knew that would have caused Most High Bodha to wonder. Her eyes searched and tried to convey reassurance to the Hu-Man before she slipped between the rocks. But what could she offer? She herself was in a poor position with the Yon-Yas. Soluma-Rah had given reluctant permission, but the decision to land truly lay on Rohongra. She acted in haste and now could be seen as having committed an act of war.

Most High Bodha led her through the abodes of the Yon-Yas to the large council chamber situated in the center of their living space. She passed the giant figurine of the prior Most High, Savat, which had been formed from Polisis. She entered their meeting chamber. They led her to the middle of the space. Around her settled the Council of Yon-Ya and their Most High Bodha. They formed an arc of seven Beings with Bodha in the middle.

Rohongra, Most High of ThAak-Too, knelt before them all.

∞-My council informs me your Beings left you here. Why?-∞

Rohongra lifted her head to the Most High. ∞-My thought leader, Dahi, has turned them from me. They believe I am at fault for the demise of ThAak-too.-∞

∞-Is that not true? Your desire for Duji was great,-∞ one of Bodha's advisors thought.

∞-No! Duji only kept those of ThAak-Too alive. We had no choice but to supply it. Without it we had no future,-∞ Rohongra argued.

∞-Your Beings had no future with it,-∞ the advisor replied.

∞-Enough,-∞ Most High Bodha cautioned. ∞-What would you have us do?-∞

Rohongra straightened her being. ∞-I want to return to my Beings. I know I can assert myself.-∞

∞-And then what?-∞ another council member thought. ∞-Where will your Beings go? What will they do? They can do naught but become slaves to Ka.-∞

Bodha raised a limb to quiet the thoughts of those around him. ∞-There is much concern over whether you would be welcomed on Celute.-∞

Rohongra jerked away. ∞-Certainly, that cannot be the case.-∞ Her eyes searched the sky above her.

∞-And what of the Hu-Mans you have brought here? Where are the others?-∞ Bodha asked.

∞-These are all that were left with me. The rest went to Celute,-∞ Rohongra acknowledged. She was in no position to take them with her, but she feared going to Celute alone. The Hu-Man, E'nov, gave her comfort.

Bodha nodded. His eyes searched hers. She looked away first, as if he'd seen too much of her.

∞-Rise, Most High,-∞ Bodha commanded.

Rohongra lifted up. She prepared her Being for the loss of life force.

Bodha moved his limb from left to right. ∞-You will return to the tors. We have much to consider.-∞

He turned and left the space, those of his council following him, until only guards surrounded her. They led her back through the abodes. Watchful eyes followed. She could not hear their thoughts.

162

Chapter 27

Mandy twirled the green leafy plant between her fingers inspecting it. In the agricultural area, she had been on her hands and knees pulling weeds for hours. Her back began to have a dull ache in the middle and her left knee hurt, but she tried hard to stay focused on the task at hand.

"Ah sure hope Evan heals soon. This job sucks," Aspen complained next to her.

Mandy nodded. She usually didn't mind being down here. It gave her time to be alone with Charlie and to think. Today, she struggled. Mandy had to agree with Aspen, she wanted Evan back to health soon. It had been almost a week since his fall and while Doc said he was better, it still prevented him from being able to work in the agricultural area.

"Ah'm not sure if ah'm pullin' the right thing," Aspen said.

"Look for the dead plants. We need to get them out, so the Co2 levels don't get too high."

"Yeah, yeah. Co2 is bad."

"How do you think it's going with only half power?" Mandy asked.

"Y'all don't seem to notice, but the animals are doin' a lot better. They've started to establish day and night patterns. We've had more consistent milk and egg production. What's this?"

"That's sweet potato. Leave it. It's not dead." Mandy's gaze found Charlie asleep a few rows away.

Aspen wrinkled her nose.

"Do you think Francine is going to be okay?" Mandy asked.

"Watcha talkin' about? She's fine."

"Well, she's been a little snippy with people lately. I'm worried the lack of coffee has caused her to change. I don't want another mean person in here."

"Ah'm sure she'll be fine. It's an adjustment for everyone. But ah do miss those snack cakes she used to serve after dinner."

Mandy involuntarily licked her lips thinking about the last Ho-Ho she had over a month ago. It had been delicious, and her mouth began watering. Now they had no more canned goods, and no meat in the freezer. They lived off porridge in the morning served with a spinach and a banana drink that only tasted good when you chugged it. Eggs, potatoes, kale and rice made up the other two meals.

A few days ago, they broke down and butchered one of the lambs because the CO_2 levels were rising. Mandy knew they could've pulled more weeds but the group voted to eat lamb. Mandy remembered that night well. Dagny hung around in the kitchen, licking her lips, rushing to help Francine prepare the sides. Aspen, on the other hand only entered right before Francine served dinner. She took her helping of salad, but refused to touch the cherry glazed yumminess. Mandy felt bad about eating it, but she couldn't help it. Her hunger wouldn't go away and Francine had used the last can of fruit they had. Mandy looked up halfway through dinner, to notice moisture around Aspen's eyes. No one else seemed to care. Even Doc broke his rule and ate meat that evening, making it all so much worse.

After that, reality quickly set in. The flour and sugar supply was low. Mandy knew Evan and Francine hoped the sugar cane they'd planted would harvest soon, but Mandy didn't think that looked too promising.

164

As their food supply shortened, Doc became even more obsessive about checking their weight. "Have you noticed how weird Doc's been lately?"

"Yeah. We need to figure out a more consistent protein supply. Y'all aren't eating another of my lambs."

Mandy shook her head. "I'd prefer if our bean plants grow fast, or the coconuts ripen, as the milk we get from them tastes like honey."

"Oh."

"I'm tired of salad with no dressing. Kale for every meal. And I'm pretty sure my skin has a tinge of orange from the sweet potatoes." Mandy held out her hand for Aspen to see, then laughed.

"What's funny?"

"My mom always said, you are what you eat. I never fully understood that statement until now." Aspen stared at her. "Well, okay I guess it's not that funny."

Aspen rose and brushed the dirt from her jeans. "Ah have to go tuck the animals in before the lights shut off for the night." Mandy nodded, but kept her head down. "Ah think it's been a positive thing, for everyone establishin' day and night routines."

"Yeah, I think it's been good, too. It makes it seem closer to our old life."

"Um, yeah," Aspen said.

"See ya." Mandy barely contained her laughter until Aspen left the room. "I know, Mom, I am what I eat." Chuckling, Mandy pushed to finish with the rest of the weeds before she'd be left in the dark.

Charlie stirred next to her, but didn't wake.

The next morning Mandy slurped her porridge. It had some weird looking fruit on top. At least Francine called it fruit. Mandy was pretty sure it wasn't fruit because Francine had told them they had run out. For all Mandy knew it could be Kale or some bug. She didn't know anymore if she would be able to tell the difference. She believed her taste buds had deadened.

"Mandy, hon, have you seen Phillip today?"

"No, but I just woke up. I've only been down to the animal pens and back." Mandy's brow furrowed. "He didn't come to dinner last night, did he?"

"That cough of his was worse at lunch. I gave him some tea to try and help soothe it, but I haven't seen him since. Perhaps I should go check on him."

"That's okay, Francine. I'll do it. You're busy." Mandy finished eating. Her stomach gurgled. She began to question the fruit while putting her dishes in the sink. They'd agreed dishes would only be done once a day. Doc said they needed to conserve water. Mandy didn't understand that, since they recycled all of the water they had everyday. But he won and now they wiped their dishes and piled them to be reused at the next meal. Mandy thought he'd started to lose it a little. She'd read how that could happen to animals in captivity. Some days he behaved caring and concerned, like when he ministered to Evan, and then other times he'd lash out. Lately she noticed everyone tiptoed around. She had a feeling something had changed, she just didn't know what.

"I'll let you know how he is when I find him," Mandy said.

She wandered through the biomes, past the savannah, and down into the mechanical room. This was Charlie's and her least favorite location. She could feel Charlie's breath on the back of her bare leg. The dark mechanical room allowed her to only see inches in front of her face.

"Phillip! Phillip, you in here?"

She heard a dry cough and then he called out. "I'm just going to lay here a few more minutes. What do you need?" Phillip attempted to sit up as she entered his room.

166

"I don't need anything. I wanted to look in on you," Mandy said.

"I think I have the flu. Need to sleep this off. Can you grab the checklist and take care of things for me?"

"Sure, Charlie and I can handle it. Right girl?" Charlie barked. "Where's the list?"

"On my desk. Ask someone to help."

Mandy hesitated in the doorway. "You sure you don't want me to get Doc?"

Phillip coughed. "Doc doesn't come down here." He seemed to force a smile to his face. "Anyway, I'm fine."

"Okay, you need anything, all you have to do is holler. The intercom down here works, right?"

Phillip nodded and dropped his head back onto the pillow.

Mandy and Charlie located the list on a clipboard, despite the mess of Phillip's desk.

"Where should we start?" Charlie answered with a bark.

They headed out. Walking through the Savannah, Mandy decided to check the length of the grass to make sure it hadn't grown too tall. Number thirty-nine on the list.

"We're already here, why waste time coming back," Mandy justified to Charlie. She took the tape measure attached to the clipboard, measured, and wrote down the length. Mandy noted it was close to its maximum height and would probably need to be cut in the next day or two.

Next, they strolled up the walk, through the doors and into the rainforest. Mandy examined the plant misters. They had kicked on and things seemed to be working well. She looked up to see the tarp they had put in place to cover the opening. It also seemed to be holding. "Let's visit the ocean." She stepped into the ocean biome, and felt more relaxed with the sound of the waves. The pumps worked fine, and the algae would not need to be cleaned off them for three days. Mandy made a note. Finally they moved through the other door that led into the lung. Charlie whined the whole way.

"Again, we're right here. We might as well take care of it." Mandy had become an expert walking down the water tube to the lung now, but she still officially listed it as her second worst place to be. The acoustics were a problem. She took in the giant concrete room with the neoprene roof. She guessed it still managed the pressure in the dome and contained enough water to use in case of a fire. However, the levels looked a little low. Mandy made another note for Phillip. She needed to ask what options they had to increase the water supply.

Mandy strolled across the room over to where the plastic tarps covered the outside door. She put on Phillip's work pants. The overalls did not fit at all, way to big and she had to find a piece of twine to tie around her waist to keep the pant legs up so she didn't trip. She also had trouble wearing his boots, but she found if she stuffed the pant legs inside them and shuffled her feet, she could get by. Finally she tied a handkerchief over her nose and mouth and put goggles over her eyes. The gas masks freaked her out. No way would she wear one.

Mandy stepped outside to see if any ash needed to be moved away from the door. Her mind wandered. She secretly hoped she wouldn't catch whatever Phillip had from wearing his clothes. He seemed really ill and it worried her.

Some ash had blown back into the alcove. Mandy pushed and shoveled it away. They couldn't afford for it to block their only exit from the Biosphere. Her gaze scanned the hills around them. Since they covered the last area of the dome, she hadn't seen the sky. She could barely distinguish between the land and air. Everything wore shades of gray.

By the time she finished, sweat stained her underarms and back. Charlie darted away as she entered the Biosphere and Mandy's hand movements kept her away.

168

Mandy took the overalls off and hung them back on their hook. "Let's go check the marsh and the crops."

The marsh looked good. The CO2 levels were normal, the mud, the correct consistency, and the animals that lived there made enough noise to wake up everything. Mandy marked it off the list. "That wasn't so bad," she said. Although she had only done this once, Mandy knew from experience Phillip made these rounds twice a day.

She picked up the pace, to match Charlie's, as they got closer to the agricultural area. Charlie bounded in, catching Aspen off guard and knocking her over from where she sat on her knees pulling weeds.

"What you up to?"

"Phillip's sick. He asked me to check the biomes."

"Oh, ah hope he's okay. He need anythin'?"

"Just sleep. Where's Dagny? Isn't she supposed to be taking this shift?"

Aspen shrugged and stretched. "You know she seems to disappear whenever it's her turn down here. I think she's sitting by the radio, waiting to hear a voice." Mandy didn't know what to say. Aspen shook her head. "Anyway, you need help?" she asked and patted Charlie's head.

"Nope, this is our last stop. I'm heading back up to let Francine know and then I'll be down to help."

"Well, what do you have to do in here?"

"It says to see if weeds need to be pulled, visit the animals and make sure they have food and water and see if the O2 levels are good."

"Everythin' seems to be workin' fine. Ah think there is a thermostat type thing over on that there wall. He writes down some numbers."

Mandy ran her finger down the list. She noticed a number at the bottom. She walked to the thermostat, wrote down the number, and moved on.

"How are the animals?" Mandy asked.

"They're a happy lot. Ah just finished feedin' them a bit ago."

"Guess I can check that off my list. See you around."

Mandy headed upstairs to let Francine know about Phillip. Then she slipped off to her bedroom for a moment. She felt sad and wanted to be alone. Poor Phillip. He did so much for them and everyone took it for granted, and yet they took over twenty-four hours to go check on him. Well, no more she thought. From now on, she'd visit him everyday. She decided to lie there for just a moment longer, but her heavy lids closed and sleep overcame her emotionally and physically exhausted body.

Chapter 28

∞

At Starlight, when Dahi resided in his private chambers away from others, he opened his thoughts to her. His Being swirled in confusion. Surprised at first, now he'd come to understand how he would use this to his benefit.

∞-I almost did not recognize your Being. The Polisis your body has gained makes you shine bright and your hair has shed its color. Only your eyes gave you away after so many moons. My Being derives great pleasure in viewing you. May I suggest you come to my chamber in haste as we have much to discuss.-∞

Dahi's large Being leaned against his cushions and waited. Dahi was most sure another war would be waged once Ka received what he needed. There had been great loss and pain during the last war. Dahi did not want to be on the wrong side this ekton. He believed all Beings were able to agree upon a collective cause of action to optimize safety, but Dahi did not believe this course of action would be chosen. His purpose and life force must remain strong.

∞-What do you want?-∞ Omis's thoughts interrupted Dahi.

∞-Your new skin has a twinge of verdant in it now. It has lost the luxurious violet it once held.-∞

∞-Yes. Is that why you requested me?-∞

∞-It used to be the proud color of your people. And your hair is white.-∞

∞-What is it your Being requires?-∞

∞-Why do you believe I want of you? I wanted your Being to be aware I noticed your changes and can see you have done well for yourself. I have heard of your many offspring with Ka. Eight, is it not? Have they been acquainted with their sister?-∞ One lip curled.

A release of air escaped Omis's throat. Dahi felt peace in his Being. He moved her thoughts close to his goal.

∞-I left and there has been no need to change that course.-∞

∞-I think our Beings are in tune with each other and our futures could be one of great success. We could plan together. I would do for you what I did for your first husband. You could be Most High.-∞

∞-I don't need you for that.-∞

∞-You have affection from the Beings of Celute. I could deliver the loyalty of the ThAak-Toons. All that stands in your way is . . .-∞

∞-Is my beloved, Most High of Celute, Ka.-∞

∞-No, not Ka. He can be managed most successfully with the right leverage. It is your female offspring that blocks your true place in the universe.-∞

Omis gave Dahi's word thought as she made her way back to Ka. Could she do as Dahi suggested? She entered Ka's space and began to prepare herself. ∞-Beloved, you have done most well,-∞ Omis purred to Ka as she drew near him.

∞-We are one.-∞ Ka pulled her close. ∞-All goes as planned. The Hu-Mans are learning, for the most part, to obey.-∞

Omis nodded and beamed. She drew away and continued her preparation. She had already placed one layer of Polisis on her body. She studied herself in the reflecting wall. Ka knew she could never own too much Polisis. The second layer waited close by. She reached for the garment at the same time as he. He took the sheath from her and then delicately dressed her. The second Polisis layer added little in weight to her body. It

172

swirled down her Being as Ka watched it settle. He felt most enamored and slid a limb over her sheath, presumably to help it lie in position. While she would never have too much Polisis, he would never have too much of her. She was his most valued possession.

∞-Some of the Hu-Mans are not submitting?-∞ she questioned.

Ka shrugged. That had been expected. Some, mostly the older ones, were set in their ways and had to be taught about submission. His Being did not fill with worry. They were, after all, Disposables. And he knew there might be more still on the Water Planet that survived. He chuckled. By the time he returned to collect more, they would readily come to him, eager to be gone from a place of destruction.

∞-If too many are handled at the same time Soluma-Rah and the council will feel their loss. They will rebuke.-∞

Ka waved a limb at his most precious. ∞-The time of Soluma-Rah is almost to an end. The time of Ka is near.-∞

Omis glided closer and touched his head with hers. ∞-Have you given more thought to exploring the galaxy for Duji? Now that ThAak-Too is no more, our power could be unlimited.-∞

Ka draped a limb over her body and caressed her. ∞-I have decided to put all efforts toward war.-∞

∞-War?-∞ Omis jerked away.

∞-I am ready to take my rightful place in the galaxy. They stopped me once before, but this time.-∞ He shook his head. ∞-I am strong.-∞

∞-You would be stronger if you controlled Duji as well as Polisis. Perhaps your idea of a two-pronged approach would be best.-∞

Ka had never discussed or thought such a thing that he could remember. He drew his brows together.

∞-Perhaps you could send Dahi and those of ThAak-Too exploring. It would keep them out of the way,-∞ she suggested.

∞-Why do you so dislike Dahi, my beloved?-∞

∞-He made me nervous when he was second to my late husband. More still when he guided my daughter into power.-∞

He pressed his Being close to hers. ∞-I could remove him from this life.-∞

Omis shook her head. ∞-I do not like him near, but feel he still has value.-∞

∞-As you wish.-∞ Ka wiped a limb across her face. ∞-Have any of the ThAak-Toons approached you?-∞

∞-I have worked to stay out of the way. It has been many solstice runs, but I fear they would recognize me.-∞

∞-And what if they did? You belong to Celute now. You are mine. The mother of our offspring. Your other life is in the past.- ∞

∞-I agree Most High, but I have found in games of power, knowledge is most valuable. I feel we would best utilize that information at some time in the future. For now, I will remain discreet.-∞

∞-I will bow to your supreme tactical knowledge. And I will send the ThAak-Toons away. However, I must warn you, Dahi is eager to attend to your daughter on Yon-Ya. If I give him his leave, he may divert and relieve her of life force.-∞

Omis shrugged.

∞-Do you not worry over her well being?-∞

∞-I worry she might halt your progress.-∞

∞-Our progress, my precious. She has no power,-∞ Ka thought.

∞-ThAak-Toon's loyalty wavers. She could become powerful once more. Her life force is one to be reckoned with.-∞

∞-I would expect nothing less. After all, she is your offspring. The desire for power must run in her center.-∞

Chapter 29

Dagny entered the tech center quietly, assuming she'd find Evan asleep. Instead, he sat with his knee up on a chair in the darkened room. She'd fought hard to have the midnight to early morning shift.

"How's it going? Hear anything good?" she asked hopefully. She'd really wanted to stay in the tech center and monitor the radio twenty-four hours a day, but Francine wouldn't hear of it. The shifts were split equally and no matter what Dagny said, Francine wouldn't budge.

"I was sitting here thinking," Evan said, "about our future. I mean we've got the turbines working, at least some of them, but it really gets you thinking about what if, doesn't it?"

Confused Dagny asked, "What if, what?"

"What if something happened to the remaining turbines? What if something happened to Phillip, who let's face it, is the only one who knows how things work around here? What if we have to be in here forever? What if our families are all dead?"

"We agreed not to think or ever talk about that stuff," Dagny snapped. "Gosh, you're sure a downer. Anything interesting come across the two-way tonight?"

"Not much. I think I had one notation all shift. Here." Evan handed her the logbook. She tried to read it in the dim light. It seemed one group updated every two hours. She wondered where they were getting their power.

Evan shook his head. "Yeah, maybe I am a bit of a downer lately. It's just this damn knee."

"It's so exciting so many people survived," Dagny said.

"So many! There's hardly anyone. At least if we're only counting those who are talking. There's small groups, but when you think of all the people in the United States, very few of us made it."

"Well, I guess I thought there wouldn't be a soul after two months, so I'm feeling like maybe there's hope."

"Sure. Hope," Evan muttered. "Listen, I'm off to bed. I'm going to try to get down to the agricultural area in the morning and see if I can do some testing on our crops. See how we're doing with oxygen. I feel bad I haven't been really able to work since my accident."

Dagny wanted to say, "Yeah, yeah, yeah," but instead helped him from the chair to his feet. "Good night," she told him and then shut the door as soon as he limped from the room.

She checked her watch, thankful her battery still worked. Everyone else's had died. She sat, the notepad ready while she waited. It should only be a few more minutes before they would report.

"This is Mountain 1. We're still here and that's all to be said tonight." She heard the static evidence they were done speaking.

"Ocean base. We lost one," the person choked and sputtered. Dagny heard weeping loud and clear before the radio connection closed.

"Ocean base, you have our sympathies. This is Red Station." Dagny waited through the long pause. She knew he wouldn't stop with that short of an update. "We still have earthquakes and aftershocks every day. Don't know if you guys are feeling them. One of our group is a geologist. He's thinking they are only 5.0 to 6.0 on the Richter scale. But as we're living underground they're frightening when they start up. I checked the logs and we haven't heard from Rushmore Central in more than twenty-four hours. If you're listening, we pray you're well."

Dagny nodded.

"Most of our group has given up hope of ever receiving help from the outside. In fact, daily I hear the discussions about how many really did survive the initial blast. Still, we wonder what our government is doing. We know The President had a bunker. We know it had all the latest in technology and we're sure they had plenty of food stored. So why haven't we heard from them. For those of us trapped by the blast zone and feeling terror daily, we're angry they don't speak up. Speak up! Tell us what happened to the East Coast. Give us hope our families may have made it. Give us hope our civilization will continue."

Dagny wiped a tear from her cheek.

"As a young man, before the blast, before the aliens, before all of this, no one could have called me a conspiracy theorist. Now? Well now, I think I'm the ringleader. I truly believe the government is safe and secure. I know they probably have plenty of clean water. Plenty of food. Plenty of fresh air. Hell, they may even have sunshine for all I know. But where are they? Why don't they acknowledge us? You don't even have to save us, just let us know what's happening. We were hit the hardest. Did anything even happen to the East Coast. If we have survivors then you know there are people east of here. Someone has to be listening. Someone has to be there."

Dagny waited patiently through a long pause. She hoped he wasn't done for the night. She could understand his frustration. The blast zone, according to everything she knew, should have taken out most of the West. Red Station must feel very cut off.

"Did anyone else think The President knew about the super volcano?" the man from Red Station went on.

Dagny nodded. She remembered how when everything had happened it had seemed the government had known.

"Did anyone else think The President knew aliens from other worlds lived out there? He gave the information about those evacuation sites rather quickly. Almost as if he'd asked those aliens to help us. Yes, the government knew about them and they kept it from us. After years of sightings. Years of calling people crazy when they thought they saw something. They pretended we were alone until this started. Then all of a sudden, there are aliens and they're here to help. And Norad, we know you're listening. Why aren't you saying anything? Why can't we hear from you? Everyone of you listening to me, you know they're listening, right?" he continued.

Dagny had forgotten to take notes and now she furiously began to scribble.

"We're surviving. We're hopeful. We're going to make it. One day, and maybe soon, we're going to walk out of here. And when we find The President, when we find the government, we'll demand answers."

This time the pause continued. The dead air frightened Dagny. The guy from Red Station usually didn't end so soon. She reached for the microphone. She wanted him to come back. To know there were others who had survived. She held the microphone to her lips, but before she could speak she heard, "This is Rushmore Central. We've got a problem. Is there a doctor out there?"

Dagny heard the request for a doctor and rose, bumping her knee on the desk. "Oh my!" She turned toward the door. Should she go and get Bolton? Dagny looked at her watch. He should be there any moment for his shift. She chewed on the pen. Her head swung toward the radio. All was quiet. Certainly other doctors had survived.

"Please, answer me," Rushmore Central asked again.

"I've sent for a nurse. She should be here soon," someone said.

The other stations were quiet. Dagny tried to relax. Surely a nurse would be able to handle the situation.

"He's running a fever and his leg is hot to the touch," Rushmore Central said. "Oh, please hurry. It's turning black and . . ." Dagny heard a hiccupping sound. "Just please."

Dagny turned. Bolton might be angry with her. They all knew how he felt about talking to the other survivors, but this seemed different. Someone clearly needed his help. She waddled to the door.

Bolton at that moment walked in. "What's wrong?" he immediately asked.

"Oh, thank goodness you're here. Someone's in trouble." Dagny took his arm and dragged him over to the radio. "You've got to help."

He pulled away. "We agreed not to communicate with the other groups. You know that."

Dagny gulped. "But." Her glance danced around the room.

"But nothing." Bolton sat in her chair. He calmly leaned his elbows on the desk, his fingers tented, and listened.

"We've a policeman on the way," one of the other groups spoke up.

"Hello," a female voice blared from the speaker. "I'm a nurse. Can you repeat what's going on?" came an answer from another group.

"One of the guys collecting fuel had a beam fall on him. His leg, his leg is all black and hot."

"Okay, it's probably just broken. Do you know how to make a splint?" the nurse said.

"No!" Bolton shook his head.

"What?" Dagny asked.

He looked up at her.

The conversation turned and all of a sudden Rushmore Central was getting ideas for objects to make a splint with.

"They've got it wrong. That guy is going to lose his leg. Maybe his life," Bolton mumbled.

"You've got to tell them," Dagny insisted.

"I don't 'got' to tell them anything," he asserted.

"He's running a fever. What can we do?" Rushmore Central asked.

The policeman came on and gave more advice.

"Stupid. They're all stupid." Bolton closed his eyes.

"Then why don't you help? Tell them."

Bolton stood and paced, while Dagny sank into the desk chair. They listened to the advice and Dagny watched as Bolton became more agitated. The two-way squawked while three different groups began to fight over the appropriate treatment.

"The leg is hard to the touch. I mean really hard," the man at Rushmore Central said.

"That's because the guy has a compression fracture," Bolton yelled at the black box. "Who are these people? They know nothing of medicine."

"One is a policeman and another a nurse. Sounds like the woman works with kids," Dagny said.

"That makes sense, because she doesn't know what the heck she's talking about."

"Well, then help them. You've got to," Dagny whined.

"He'll be better once the leg is set," the police officer said.

"No he won't. He'll probably die. Best case, he'll just lose his leg," Bolton said.

Dagny bowed her head. On the radio, in the background, she could hear the screaming of the man.

"Stop! Stop right now!" Bolton finally yelled into the microphone.

* * *

Mandy rushed into the kitchen. Her wet hair pulled back in a band, hung barely dry. She had just stepped out of the shower when she heard Francine's voice over the intercom asking for the emergency meeting. Mandy wasn't sure what had happened but it couldn't be good. She saw Aspen and Evan walk in behind her.

"Bolton saved that person, Francine," Dagny pleaded. "The guy would've died but for him." Mandy looked at Doc, who had a very smug smile on his face.

"I'm not opposed to him saving people. However, we agreed on two things as a group. Both were on your agenda, Doctor. One, someone needed to be in charge so people didn't go off and make bad decisions that risked the lives of those in the group and two, we shouldn't talk on the two-way because it jeopardized us. You completely risked our safety for your own gain."

"Francine, we had no time," Dagny, defended, while Doc stood across the room, a scowl firmly in place.

"Um, I don't mean to interrupt, but can somebody tell me what's going on?" Mandy asked.

"An injured man needed help. They asked on the radio if anyone had a doctor. Bolton saved the guy's life," Dagny said.

"Other people acted like idiots. They would've killed him," Doc said.

"That's not the point," Francine yelled. "It's about the safety of our group. And Bolton didn't do it to save another's life." She turned to him. "You did it to prove how right and good you are. All I'm saying is we should've made a group decision."

"Francine, no matter Doc's reasons, he had to step in. It was the right thing to do," Evan said.

"Ah'm sorry y'all. Ah disagree. He shouldn't have jumped in. He risked our safety for the benefit of one. He should've at least asked what we thought."

Phillip coughed in the corner, interrupting their argument for a moment. Mandy didn't think he looked well. She was surprised he had even felt well enough to get up. She turned to look at Doc, wondering if he even had noticed it had been her that had covered for Phillip the last few days. She felt grateful Doc lived in the Biosphere with them, but hoped he'd soon realize Phillip had to be treated.

"You should spend your time helping Phillip, if you need to do something," Francine said as she slammed a cupboard, echoing Mandy's thought moments before.

"Phillip, go to the medical center," Doc ordered.

Mandy felt bad for Phillip. As their most valuable team member it must have felt awful being sick and ordered around, treated like a toddler. Phillip ignored Doc and continued to stand in place. Mandy suspected he would've liked to leave but stayed to defy the man.

"Francine, you're being ridiculous right now," Dagny argued." What if it was your daughter he saved?"

"We made the rules together. We agreed upon them as a group and although I may have made the choice to step in and help, the point is we didn't get to choose because Bolton went behind everyone's back and made the choice for us," Francine argued. "No one should act without group knowledge and one person shouldn't make the choice to risk all of our lives. We have to be accountable to each other before we're accountable to others. And if we can't trust or communicate with each other, we jeopardize everyone."

"You have a fantastic flare for the dramatic," Doc spat. "I didn't risk anyone's life. I saved a life, remember?"

"Who did you say you were?" Mandy asked.

"I never said my name or where we lived. I told them I had a medical degree and I knew how to save the man if someone competent enough could follow my directions."

Mandy's jaw dropped. How could anyone be so arrogant? She wondered why anyone even listened to him.

"Francine, circumstances change. Someone's life hung in the balance," Mandy said. "There may be more people that need a doctor. They know we exist and eventually they're going to start asking questions. What do we tell them?"

Phillip tried to suppress another cough.

"I need to get Phillip checked out." Doc rose to leave.

"Before you go, you're on radio silence till we can decide as a group how much to share," Francine said. She turned on her heel and over her shoulder said, "Dagny, I'm relieving you of radio duties, too. Mandy, please cover Dagny's shift and Evan you take Bolton's. They can pick up more shifts weeding the crops."

Mandy nodded and quickly left, not wanting to hang around. She understood Francine being upset, and suspected her motive as trying to rein Doc in. She couldn't believe Francine didn't want Doc to help that guy. At least Mandy hoped she wasn't that callous. At the moment though, she made Doc look like the nice one. Mandy shuddered at the thought. She missed her brother and her parents even more now that her new family was unraveling under the pressure.

Chapter 30

∞

Dahi's litter moved through the gathering place. His eyes flittered from face to face. Where did his most trusted allies go? He caught sight of them and directed his handlers to take him closer. When they neared, his Beings bowed low. Dahi's grin spread wide. It was as it should be. His garments did not compare to anyone else's. They hung from his large frame lavishly reminding those around him of the years in power he'd served.

His carriers lowered him to the surface of the planet. He motioned for them to back away. He nodded to the trusted. ∞-Come to me,-∞ he beckoned. Eight Beings gathered around him. ∞-We have been given instructions from Ka.-∞ Not a one made a move. ∞-We have been ordered to search the galaxy for Duji.-∞

The Being on his right limb, huffed and then spat on the planet. ∞-Of course. We should go immediately and find a new source,-∞ he thought.

∞-You are right. Ka wishes us to go out and away. However, Ka is not Most High of ThAak-Toons.-∞ Dahi read the thoughts of those around him and knew his eyes glittered.

∞-Even Most High Rohongra is not our leader,-∞ The others' thoughts came to him. ∞-You are.-∞

∞-If that were so, I would not obey Ka. I would send a group to find Rohongra. Find her and remove her claim to Most High.-∞ Dahi waited. The thoughts around him stilled. Not since the war had any Being endangered another. He could wait. They must reach their own truths. He turned to wave over his handlers, but the Being to his right stopped him.

∞-It would be necessary to release her life force.-∞ The Being tested those around him.

Dahi nodded. He worked to contain his glee.

∞-It is never good to lose life force,-∞ another thought came to them.

∞-You are correct. It is not a good thing.-∞ Dahi patted the pillows beneath his limbs. ∞-If only she hadn't urged our Beings deeper and deeper into ThAak-Too. Now I can no longer testify to her thoughtfulness.-∞

∞-Ka will not accept this well. He is one to be wary of.-∞

∞-Wary, yes, but not fearful.-∞ Dahi leaned his huge form forward. ∞-He has no authority over our Beings. We could separate. Two of our discs could go out as Ka suggested, and two to first attend to our Most High Rohongra.-∞ His thoughts slid through the minds of those around. They nodded. ∞-Can I trust you to handle the details?-∞ He turned to the Being at his right.

A quick nod.

∞-I will join those who go to Yon-Ya, but first I have something to attend to.-∞ Dahi motioned to his handlers. They lifted and carried him away.

* * *

Ektons later, Omis' eyes widened as Dahi entered her presence. ∞-I did not summon you.-∞ Her head turned away from him.

∞-I will leave you soon. I am going to attend to your daughter on Yon-Ya.-∞

Omis swiveled in her seat. ∞-You were informed you should leave to find Duji. My most precious will not be pleased you disobey.-∞

Dahi's face squinted. ∞-Ka is not my Most High. I must attend to Rohongra before I can give my allegiance to any Being.-∞

∞-Your allegiance?-∞

Dahi pointed his stubby limb at her.

Chapter 31

Bolton stomped away from the dining room with Phillip trailing behind. Francine's need to control everything made him furious. How ridiculous. He'd saved someone's life. He did a good deed and could she be happy? No. She had to have something to attack him about. Phillip's cough brought him back to the present.

They entered the medical center and Bolton motioned for Phillip to sit on the end of the patient bed. "I really don't understand why Francine has to try to tell everyone what to do. I mean really. You'd think she'd be glad I saved someone. That I'm showing my caring side. Jeez, she has to be the most - hold your arm out - infuriating woman ever."

Bolton took a breath while Phillip held out his arm. He put on the blood pressure cuff, squeezed the bulb and released the pressure.

"This time I agree with you."

Bolton smiled. "Thank you. I share my talent and skills with someone and the woman feels she has the right to be indignant. How's your urination?"

"Excuse me?"

"Your urination? How is it looking? Does it burn? Is it a strong stream or does it trickle out? Any blood?"

"I'm fine."

Bolton nodded. Not sure if his patient told the truth. If he practiced in his high tech hospital where he should be, a low level assistant would be doing this and he'd be drinking a cup of coffee and reading the latest medical research. Why, he wondered, had he ever decided to take this job in the first place? He shrugged. Of course, if he hadn't come here he'd probably be wandering around searching for his next meal. "How about excretions?" he asked.

Phillip looked at Bolton, no response forthcoming quickly. He decided to clarify. "Any discharge from your…?"

"No." Color rose to Phillip's cheeks.

"How about bowel movements? Soft or hard, dark colored? Does it float or sink."

"Fine."

"Any fever or night sweats?"

"No."

"Well that's good because if you had those, I'd be very worried." He ran a hand through his hair. Bolton took his stethoscope and listened to Phillip's chest. Very little air moved through his lungs. He bit his lower lip. "Do you have a plutonic cough?" Phillip once again stared blankly at him. "A tight sharp pain in the chest when you cough, or is it dry and you feel hoarse?"

"Sharp pain."

"Take another deep breath." Phillip inhaled and coughed. Bolton jumped back in time for Phillip to get his mouth covered. Bolton turned away and immediately went to the sink to wash his hands. Before he returned to Phillip's side, he'd placed a mask over his own mouth and nose. He pulled out a pair of latex gloves and shoved his hands into them. Out of the corner of his eye he saw Phillip shove a towel into his pocket. He wandered over to a cupboard and opened it. He had no reason to look inside, he just couldn't figure out what to do next. He turned. "Blood?" Bolton asked.

"What?"

"Did you have blood in your phylum just now?" Phillip began to cough again. Bolton sighed. He noticed when Phillip inhaled, his brows furrowed and his lips pulled tightly together.

188

"It hurts when you breathe. Can you even take a full breath?"

Phillip shook his head. "It's hard."

Bolton bit his lower lip. What was wrong? "How are you sleeping?"

"I can't."

He tilted his head to one side.

"My throat burns," Phillip admitted.

"Since when?"

"Now."

"Body aches, on a scale of one to ten?"

"Four."

Bolton moved around the room. He approached and pinched Phillip's arm.

"Ouch."

"Sorry. You're very dehydrated. Hop on the scale. I really think the only reason Francine disagrees with what I did is because she didn't come up with the idea herself. Here drink this. I mean who would've thought Francine would be opposed? You've dropped weight. Oxygen level. Hold still. I mean, really it might be better for us if later on we have something to trade. We might need food or grain and we can trade that for medical care. I don't think she's smart enough to see the big picture. Your oxygen levels are very low. That is really bad, Phillip." Bolton stood stunned. He had no idea what he was dealing with. Or how long had passed since Phillip became sick. Was it days? Or a week? With everything going on, he'd been remiss in checking vitals and recording the findings. " Do you feel light-headed?"

"No."

"Not even a little?"

"Sometimes."

"Your lungs sound bad. They're clogged. No air moving in and out of them. Your BMI and weight have dropped significantly. And, I noticed some blood on your teeth. When did you start having blood in your sputum?"

"After we were in the turbines."

"This could be a couple of different illnesses. None of them are good, living in the conditions here. You didn't take your mask off right? So, I really don't think it's something you inhaled. Let me check one more thing. You can sit down."

Bolton moved away from Phillip. "Do you think we could get Evan and Aspen to see how bad things are with Francine in charge? Get them and Mandy to vote against Francine?"

Something crashed behind him. Bolton turned in time to see Phillip's head bounce off the floor.

* * *

Mandy stood in the kitchen helping Francine prepare lunch.

"Man y'all, my body hurts today," Aspen said as she plopped down on a stool. Mandy stood next to her.

"Yeah, the blisters on my fingers, have grown blisters," Mandy said as Evan joined them at the counter. She sighed. Her clothes hung on her. The low calorie diet didn't give her the energy to get through the day.

Doc had gone to the medical center he said to check Phillip's cough, but Mandy knew he pouted. Francine once again had out-smarted and out-manned him. Mandy thought about how she hoped Phillip would feel better soon. He did so much for them in the dome. Mandy knew that from having taken over for him. It was back breaking work.

"I need help in the med center!" Doc's obnoxious voice boomed over the intercom, interrupting lunchtime. He probably needed help moving the bike or other such nonsense, Mandy thought.

190

Charlie barked.

"Phillip's fallen down," he said. "He's unconscious. Hurry!"

Mandy ran with the others at her heels. She rounded the corner, entered the medical center door and found Phillip lying on the floor. Doc had him on his side. Mandy gasped. She covered her mouth, took a step towards Phillip, and knelt by him. He breathed erratically and his eyelids fluttered but didn't open.

Tears filled her eyes. She felt a presence behind her and turned to see Francine. She wasn't an incredibly religious person, but suddenly she found herself bargaining with God. "Please," Mandy whispered.

Francine reached out and touched Phillip's cheek.

When Evan entered the medical center, everyone else stood in a circle around Phillip and Doc.

"Is he breathing?" Dagny asked wide-eyed.

"Barely," Doc said. He knelt beside the larger man. "I need him on his side so he doesn't choke."

"What happened?" Francine asked.

"His oxygen level is low. He's coughing up blood. I need help to get him on the bed. He's heavy. It'll take all of us to lift him." Doc wore gloves and a mask. He hurried to a cabinet and grabbed a gown to complete his outfit.

Together they lifted and placed Phillip on the bed.

"Get a blanket," Francine ordered.

Evan grabbed one from the cupboard and covered Phillip. "You'll be okay," he said. Evan felt helpless and scared. He wished his mother, the physician, were there. "What else can we do?

Doc shook his head. "Stand back. I don't know if he's contagious."

"What?" Dagny said, her mouth falling open.

Doc lifted his palms. "I don't know what's wrong. There are several possibilities. None good. And I don't have the right equipment to figure it out. We've no choice, but hope his body can fight it."

Evan closed his eyes. His hands trembled.

Doc glanced around. "I don't have any way of knowing. This could be environmental or it could be a bacterial infection." He rubbed the back of his neck.

Evan's mouth felt dry and he wiped his hands on his pants as he paced. A sound interrupted his thoughts. Francine sobbed.

Doc quickly moved across the room, pushed Phillip onto his back and started pounding on his chest. "Get me the ambu bag!" he screamed.

Evan's mind raced. He didn't understand what Doc needed. "What?"

Doc motioned toward a cupboard. Evan dashed to it, found a bag and mask and ran it to the table. Doc grabbed the mask, put it over Phillip's mouth and began pumping air into his lungs. "Here, help me." Aspen stepped close and squeezed the bag while Doc thumped on Phillip's chest. Minutes ticked by. Evan held his breath.

"Come on. Breathe," Aspen said.

Doc suddenly stopped and turned away. Evan's gaze found Aspen across the table. Her eyes contained moisture. Phillip was gone.

Chapter 32

∞

∞-Welcome, Most High.-∞ Soluma-Rah's Second-in-command, Gramar acknowledged her presence in the holding area. He had supervised the unloading and trade of life-sustaining and beautifying materials. ∞-Our goods are much attenuated this time.-∞

∞-That reduction was anticipated,-∞ she thought. ∞-I feel great turmoil around us, and unrest in the council. What are those who trade, thinking? What knowledge has been shared during the transfers?-∞

∞-Ka's planet has sent the thought leader of ThAak-Too in search of Duji. The ones who bring Polisis fear he is moving to control all.-∞

∞-This has been his goal for many ektons.-∞

∞-Yes, but Most High, he is working with others now,-∞ Gramar informed her.

Soluma-Rah believed knowledge of a certain kind had been hidden from her. ∞-Please share all.-∞ She sensed his hesitation. Her thoughts delved into his mind.

Finally, he opened to her. ∞-Most High Ka and Omis are said to be working with Dahi to rid Rohongra of life force.-∞

∞-I see,-∞ Soluma-Rah thought.

∞-He might gain enough power to control others and eventually, it is feared, turmoil and unrest will cause the loss of your position as well.-∞

Soluma-Rah finally had all the pieces. Now, she understood the hesitation of her council. This latest news did not surprise, but she considered it most unwelcome. She kept her thoughts private. No reason to worry her Beings.

∞-What news do you have of Rohongra?-∞

∞-Most High Bodha has safely returned to Yon-Ya with no Hu-Mans in his holds. Rohongra's future has not been decreed by his council yet. And if Most High Bodha has made a decision, he has not yet shared it.-∞

∞-Most High.-∞ Her Second thought. ∞-News travels to us. Ka has prepared his ships.-∞

∞-For what?-∞

∞-Those who trade do not have the exact knowledge. They saw ships equipped to travel.-∞

Soluma-Rah nodded. This new information did not quell her inner angst. ∞-We must continue to prepare our Beings.-∞

∞-Yes, Most High.-∞

∞-Where are we with training the Hu-Mans.-∞

∞-They show great strength and determination. Together they have learned the use of some of our devices. We believe they are able to move as one, contributing to the success and protection of their life force.-∞

∞-Is our protective field ready?-∞

∞-Yes. If Ka's ships enter our airspace we will have enough warning. We continue to prepare underground for protection of our non-fighting Beings. We also have gathered and stored all available weapons.-∞

∞-It brings my Being great sadness we are once again priming for affray. Have we not learned from our past this only ends in tragedy for all?-∞ Soluma-Rah thought.

∞-We hold a belief, Most High Ka and his most precious, Omis, must be stripped of all power in order for peace to be re-established.-∞

She inhaled. ∞-We have always allowed choice for all Beings.-∞

194

∞-Most High, there may be no other way to gain peace.-∞

Soluma-Rah stepped out of her council chambers. She hated to think controlling choices of another planet would be a possible solution. Beings should be free to choose who ruled them. The collective agreement established protection for all. There were proper channels guided by mutual agreement. If Beings showed distress from those who led, options existed. She refused to believe after all this time they could abandon this principle. Soluma-Rah disliked giving in to forced manipulation of Beings over free choice.

* * *

Soluma-Rah's image coalesced on the screen in front of Bodha. He nodded in deference. ∞-Most High Elected.-∞

∞-I am pleased with your return to Yon-Ya,-∞ she acknowledged. ∞-My thoughts cause me to twist and turn. Your planet harbors Rohongra.-∞

∞-She is a fellow Most High,.-∞ Bodha lifted his limbs, ∞-and we are peaceful Beings.-∞

∞-I acknowledge that truth. But you have put others at risk,-∞ Soluma-Rah thought. ∞-Those who transport Polisis have spoken of Ka. He has joined with Dahi.-∞ Soluma-Rah leaned closer to her console. ∞-Dahi will have to remove Rohongra's life force. It will prove his loyalty to Ka. Your planet, your Beings are in danger.-∞

Bodha released breath.

∞-We have enjoyed peace, but there will be no more. Ka wants power. Without Duji . . . -∞ Soluma-Rah's thoughts were clear.

Bodha's eyes searched for an answer. ∞-What do you advocate?-∞

∞-We must head off the invaders and give Ka no reason to attack your planet at this time. The best resolution is to release Rohongra's life force.-∞

Bodha gazed at his appendages. ∞-You ask the impossible.-∞

∞-The rest of The Federation must hold them off long enough to unify. There is truth in this.-∞

∞-I cannot align with that thought.-∞

∞-Your Beings can afford no other choice.-∞ Soluma-Rah's presence flickered and became lost.

Bodha's private thoughts raced. He quickly requested his council's appearance. ∞-Dahi and Ka prepare for war,-∞ his thoughts invaded those surrounding him.

All eyes shifted to the sky. If affray came again, they would be the first to know.

∞-The Most High of ThAak-Too must be evacuated at once. As should the rest of the Hu-Mans.-∞ Momur, standing beside him, shivered.

∞-What of the rest who dwell here? Where do we go?-∞ One of his council inquired.

∞-Once Rohongra and the Hu-Mans have been transported, there will be no reason for conflict.-∞

∞-And what if Dahi and Ka are already on their way? What if they come before you return?-∞

∞-You shall advise them Rohongra has escaped-∞

Bodha inclined his head and Momur brought forth the Most High of ThAak-Too. Rohongra entered their council, her spine straight and her head aloft. She floated to the center of the area, as if aware her fate would soon be decided.

∞-Most High Rohongra, your Beings are in revolt. They have joined Celute and are coming for you.-∞

Rohongra's eyes grew wide but then quickly narrowed. ∞-I will await them.-∞ She nodded, resigned.

∞-No, you will prepare to leave Yon-Ya immediately.-∞
Bodha waved a limb at Momur. ∞-The discs are ready?-∞

∞-What of the Hu-Mans? They are in danger.-∞

∞-The Hu-Mans await you. All of you must leave. Your council is no more. All that remain are those who are loyal to Dahi and Ka as leaders.-∞ Bodha regretted having to be so blunt. It was not his nature. ∞-Enough. We leave now. And perhaps it will mean the survival of all.-∞

Chapter 33

Bolton watched as Dagny stumbled out of the medical center.

Phillip's bowels had evacuated and the stench in the small area permeated everything. Bolton would have liked to also leave, but he had work to do. Francine, unable to control her tears, had also slipped out of the room. This left him with only a few crowding around.

"Ah can't believe he's dead," Aspen said.

Mandy sniffled in the corner, her head on Evan's shoulder.

"I need to do an autopsy. You should leave," Bolton said to them. What had happened? He couldn't believe he hadn't been able to save Phillip. His palms sweated and he wiped his brow.

"Don't defile him. It isn't right," Mandy said.

"How are we going to bury him?" Evan asked. "There's ten or more feet of solidified ash everywhere outside." He released Mandy and stepped closer.

"We could put him in the base of one of the broken turbines," Bolton said. "But first I need to know what killed him. Then we can carry him wherever you want." Bolton gathered instruments and laid them out on the counter close by, knives and saws that he removed from drawers and cupboards, a staple gun, and finally a large number of towels. He blinked several times. How could Phillip have died on his watch?

"I can't believe we're letting him do this," Mandy said. "It's wrong."

Aspen shook her head. "No. Doc is right. We need to know what killed Phillip."

"But we can't leave his body in the base of a turbine. He deserves a burial," Mandy argued.

"There's no where to bury him. We'd need a jackhammer to break through all the ash. The acid rain has turned it into concrete," Evan said. "We'd never be able to get through it.

Aspen turned away and blew her nose.

"You all need to leave now," Bolton interrupted their discussion. He didn't care about anything but why Phillip had died, and they were holding him up from finding out. Mandy turned and left with Evan and Charlie following.

Bolton heard the door clink shut behind them. He didn't look up until he heard the pounding on the window that separated them. That's when he noticed Aspen had locked herself in with him. "No!" Evan rapped on the Plexiglas. Aspen looked at him. "I'm staying," she said.

"I don't need your help. You can leave. It probably would be better if you did."

"You'll need help. Ah'm your best option. Besides, I agree with Mandy, we shouldn't defile his body any more than necessary."

"Put some stuff on if you're staying. Gown, mask and gloves." Bolton picked up the sharpest knife and began to cut. A moment later he looked into Aspen's unmasked face. Phillip's bodily fluids began to seep around the knife and out of his skin. He looked up. Aspen's face was stone. He kept going until just below the belly button. Phillip's ribs had been cracked during CPR, making it easier for Bolton to pull them apart. Both he and Aspen leaned in.

"What is that?" Aspen asked.

Bolton shook his head. A spongy substance covered the bottom lung and fuzz had spread to his heart. He poked the material with the tip of his knife. Bolton gasped and moved back from the particles floating up. Spreading. Bile rose in his throat. He forced himself to take deep breaths to calm himself.

"Close him up, close him up," Aspen yelled.

Bolton moved into overdrive. He grabbed his staple gun and quickly began the tedious process of stretching the skin back together.

"Help. This will go faster if you hold his skin and I staple." Bolton looked up. "Aspen hurry," he said. Her skin had become the color of ash.

She nodded. When he began to staple he saw Aspen's hands shaking a little, but her color returned and she looked visibly calmer.

* * *

Dagny shivered and pulled a blanket tighter around her shoulders. Any moment someone would be there to take over. In fact, it wasn't even her shift. She would've given anything for chocolate, but her candies were long gone. How could Phillip be dead?

The radio squawked. She sank into her chair, numb. What would they do? Phillip knew the most about the Biosphere. With him dead, they didn't stand a chance of surviving there.

"This is Delta Sweet. We wanted to let everyone know, we've added to our numbers. Two groups from across the mountains met up and made their way here. We're excited. One is a carpenter, and the other, an engineer. They've got ideas for a water system. They even brought some seed."

Dagny listened intently. Survivors were coming together. She leaned forward, as if it would bring her nearer to the others. Her fingers itched to pick up the microphone. She wanted details. How had she not heard of survivors traveling across the mountains before? Tears slid down her cheeks. Angry, she wiped them away.

She heard a sound and turned to the door. No one entered. For all she knew, they could all still be standing in the medical center. Her chest heaved. She had no doubt, whatever Phillip had, would probably spread.

Dagny rose from her chair. Her eyes scanned the room. She had a backpack somewhere. If others were able to cross the land, why couldn't she? Her mother referred to her as sturdy. And young. Twenty-three. She could do it. If only she had a map. Her mind raced. But the landmarks would be different since the eruption. A map wouldn't help. Heck, what did they use in the old days? She needed a compass. Yes, a compass. Vaguely, she remembered how once in science class she'd made one using a needle and water? How had she put it all together? If only she had access to the Internet. This whole business was getting to be too much. How could one live without information?

She could leave. Just walk on out of there. She found a slip of paper and began to write notes. Her hand found the process unfamiliar. Several times she scratched out words. Food came first on the list. She'd have to pack lots of food. And a blanket. She wouldn't take any clothes. No, she'd need to travel light. She stood. Just food, oh and water. She looked around and the tears flowed freely. She'd die. She'd either die here or out there.

Dagny sat and let her head drop to the desk.

"This is Rushmore Central. We heard the good news." A long pause followed. "We're happy to hear others have joined you." Dagny heard a choking sound. Something was wrong. She sat back and let her head loll. They, too, had been faced with sickness. She waited to hear the news of one more death or illness.

She looked at her list. Her shoulders shook. She'd never make it. She had no idea how to survive.

Dagny picked up the microphone. Her fingers trailed along the button. She considered what would happen if anyone found out.

* * *

Mandy stood on Evan's left. A head taller, he could easily see into the small window of the medical center door. "How are things going?" she whispered. He stared at her a moment before answering.

"Not good. Something happened. They've been frantic ever since. They stapled Phillip up, stuffed him in a bag, and now they're disinfecting every surface."

Mandy rose on her tiptoes and tried to see through the window. "What do you think it means?" He wasn't telling her something. "Why are they acting so weird?" she asked.

"I don't know, haven't you been listening to me?" Evan snapped at her. "Something happened. Doc opened him up. They leaned in. They jumped back. It's been crazy ever since."

"Why don't we try and get in?"

"The door is locked. I tried it."

"What do we do?"

"I don't know," Evan said.

Mandy couldn't imagine what could cause such a strong reaction from Doc and Aspen, but she guessed it wasn't good. What had happened? Even on her tiptoes she had trouble seeing into the room. Her eyes burned and she blinked several times before rubbing them.

"Aspen shouldn't have stayed. I knew it was a bad idea, but no one ever listens to me," he said, with closed eyes and his head resting against the wall.

Francine touched Mandy's arm. "What's going on?" she asked.

202

"Aspen locked herself in with Doc. They're doing an autopsy. Something happened." Tears sprang to her eyes.

When she looked over at Evan she noticed his eyes were wet too. He wiped them away.

"It'll be okay, Evan," Mandy said. She gave him a hug. Charlie sniffed at the door and pawed. She didn't really believe what she told him.

"Bolton knows what he's doing. You'll see Evan," Francine assured him.

Evan shook his head. Mandy didn't know what had happened, but even she didn't believe Doc would be able to fix this. Her body felt numb.

Evan pushed Francine away from the window and peered in. "Aspen is sobbing," he reported. "And Doc is leaning against the wall. His shoulders are shaking. I think he's crying, too."

Francine placed a hand out to move Evan back. She looked through the window for a moment and then walked away. Mandy didn't know what to think, what to do. She slid to the floor, her back against the wall and dropped her head into her hands.

* * *

Bolton wiped the wall to the left of Phillip's body. He didn't know if he and Aspen did any good, but he needed to do something.

"What was that stuff?" Aspen had asked him, over and over.

He had no answers. He had failed. It looked like mold, but the consistency and color were off. The green spots on Phillip's lower lung and the white ones on his heart were spongy looking, slimy and translucent.

"I don't want to die," she whispered.

203

"Me either. When we finish, we'll bag our clothes. Hopefully our masks protected us."

"But I didn't have one on when you opened him. I didn't put it on until later," Aspen said.

Bolton didn't know what to say to that. It worried him. She had stood too close when he opened Phillip. He warned her. Now he wanted to shout, but what good would that do?

"What about the others? The biosphere?" Aspen asked. "Do you think the others are in danger?"

"I don't know. Just keep cleaning. That's where we need to focus our energy."

Bolton turned away from Aspen. He was tired, frustrated and completely perplexed by his discovery. And nervous. Would his mask even protect him? He glanced at Aspen.

"We should've left his body alone," she murmured.

Bolton picked up the disinfectant bottle from the counter and began to wipe each instrument again. He contemplated throwing them all in the bag with Phillip, but thought he might need them. He slowed, making sure he sterilized each instrument thoroughly. He glanced up from time to time. Several times he caught Evan looking in.

"You shower first. I'll bag up everything. When you're finished, put on this garbage bag. I cut a hole in the top for your head."

"It's a garbage bag," Aspen said. Her lower lip trembled.

"Yes. I put a hole in it."

"But it's a garbage bag."

"It's all we have right now. I'll ask the others to get you a change of clothes."

Aspen turned and headed toward the back of the medical center. Bolton knew he would be bombarded with questions when he opened the door. He stood still trying to put all the pieces together. None of it made sense.

Mandy walked down the hallway in a daze. She went to find Francine to let her know they would do a service for Phillip once Doc and Aspen finished.

She found the former housemother in her bedroom. Francine stared out the window, but turned when she heard Mandy enter. Her eyes were red and swollen, and she mumbled to herself.

"Hi." Francine's lips turned up slightly, but stopped there. She rubbed the fingers of one hand against Mandy's cheeks. It felt awkward and Mandy moved back a little.

"We're going to have a service for Phillip before we take him out," Mandy said. She found it hard to focus.

Francine began to gulp in air, and then loud sobs racked her frame.

"I know it's not great, but there's really no other way," Mandy said.

Francine nodded. She attempted to compose herself.

"Remember how heavy Phillip was? Evan's sure it's going to require all of us to move his body downstairs," she said.

Francine had tears running down her cheeks.

"My daughter." Francine reached for her hand.

"Um, what?" Mandy stepped closer, confused. "Your daughter?"

"I need to try and find her. If Phillip died . . . well, I don't want to die without saying good-bye. What if she's out there? She could be suffering. She could be waiting for me to come and find her." A sound gurgled in her throat. She covered her mouth with one hand.

Mandy sighed. She felt the same way about her brother and Jesse. "No one else is going to die."

Francine's sobs grew louder.

Mandy stood next to the bed and shuffled her feet. She wiped her hands on her pants. "We should go. You should say good-bye."

Francine's grief suffocated her. "How about I meet you there?"

Mandy turned and ran out the room and down the hallway to rid herself of the feelings.

Chapter 34

∞

∞-Most High,-∞ one of Ka's Beings cautiously approached him. ∞-I have thought.-∞ They stood beside one of the Celute transportation discs. They readied for something more than just travel.

∞-Soluma-Rah has activated her planet's shields.-∞

Ka grinned. So Soluma-Rah would be the one to start conflict. He spit. Well, she could start the affray. He would finish it. ∞-How are the Hu-Man warriors? Are they ready?-∞

∞-Many have become quite adept at using our armaments. The older ones. They will increase our force greatly. The young have been found to be of little use.-∞

∞-To be expected. But it is good. A strong first wave of defense.-∞

His Being nodded, but the thought came, ∞-If there were more, our success would be sure.-∞

∞-Prepare two more of our ships to leave immediately. We shall go to gather Hu-Mans. This time we will collect all who remain. There are still strong life forces emanating from there.-∞

Ka hastened away, his Being pleased with what he saw. The design for his ultimate authority was within reach. Even Dahi and his Beings fell into place with their quest for Duji. He would soon be Most High Elected of The Federation.

∞-I'm preparing to depart.-∞ He strode into Omis's presence.

∞-I have heard Soluma-Rah prepares for affray. You cannot leave. Not now.-∞ Omis gripped one of his limbs.

Ka flung her off. ∞-Do not presume too much.-∞ He saw the surprise in her eyes and immediately quieted. ∞-There is nothing to worry about. I've sent Dahi and his Beings away, and Soluma-Rah will not act without cause. I will go collect more Hu-Mans and when I return, we shall become one again.-∞

∞-Dahi goes to Yon-Ya.-∞ Omis kept her distance. ∞-He goes to remove Rohongra's life force.-∞

∞-So? Do you have feelings for your offspring?-∞ Ka's brows rose.

∞-He is clearing the way for you,-∞ Omis thought.

∞-He disobeys me? I ordered him to find Duji.-∞ Ka swirled. ∞-If he goes to Yon-Ya, he will begin the war Soluma-Rah looks for.-∞

Omis nodded and moved closer. She inclined her head to his. ∞-And you should punish him.-∞

∞-Once I am Most High Elected many will be punished. But now is not the time. I have much to accomplish first.-∞

∞-As always, your thoughts are one with mine.-∞

* * *

Dahi's transportation disc landed and his eyes searched the planet beyond. How could the Beings of Yon-Ya be so stupid as to allow his disc to ground? He waved a hand and bearers lifted his chair. ∞-Take me to their council.-∞

The Beings of ThAak-Too glided effortlessly across the open space not seeing a single Being from Yon-Ya alight to welcome them.

∞-Are there no warriors?-∞ he ridiculed.

As they entered the central courtyard, Dahi and his Beings finally found those who inhabited the planet.

∞-Beings,-∞ he acknowledged. ∞-I must have council with Most High Bodha. We have come for Rohongra.-∞ The

Beings of Yon-Ya shifted to guide his bearers to where the council stood.

Dahi motioned his Beings to lay the chair down.

He struggled to gain his limbs beneath him, he wanted to tower above them and show his strength. ∞-I have come for Rohongra. Release her to me.-∞

∞-Supreme Thought Leader, we do not have her.-∞ The Being who came forward was quickly flung to the ground by Dahi's Second.

∞-Do not approach in such a manner. Bow before him.-∞ The Second raised a limb and threatened. Dahi watched as the Beings quietly settled on the planet in front of him.

They would be easy to control. He sneered. ∞-I repeat. I want Rohongra brought to me,-∞ he thought.

Not one of the Beings lifted their minds to thought.

∞-This is an act of war. You have kept our Most High a prisoner on your planet.-∞ Dahi waddled back and forth in front of the Beings.

∞-It is an act of war for you to land on our planet,-∞ the thought came quietly.

Dahi shifted to see them all.

A younger Being rose before him. ∞-Your Most High Rohongra does not reside here. She left the planet with the Hu-Mans. We do not know where they have gone.-∞

Another Being lifted from the ground. ∞-We should all share thought with the Most High Elected.-∞

Dahi swirled. ∞-Soluma-Rah's authority over the galaxy is no longer recognized by me or mine. She is the reason ThAak-Too is no more and we have to rely on the kindness of Celute. She and the greed of those of the Astral Zone.-∞

∞-Supreme Thought Leader, we are peaceful Beings. We wish you well on your journeys to finding your leader, but we have no knowledge.-∞ Another Being rose from the dirt.

Dahi twisted. His scream caused them to cower. ∞-Where is your Most High? Where is Bodha? Where does he hide?-∞ He took turns towering over each risen Being until they all resumed a position of inferiority. They were so easy to control.

* * *

Rohongra glided through the transportation disc. Dismayed by its antiquated technology, she'd forgotten how Yon-Ya had remained silent during the war, refusing to take sides or participate in any manner. Still she had thought they'd be able to protect themselves adequately. Now she knew the truth. They were weak. They only had Ten-Dati to save them.

She slipped into the presence of Bodha. His vision focused on the darkness surrounding them. Far in the distance she could see the sparkling of planets and stars, the galaxy unfamiliar to her. She startled. Where had he decided to take her?

∞-If you really wanted to return to your Beings, you could have sent thought to them.-∞ Bodha didn't turn, though he acknowledged her.

Rohongra knew he was precise. She could have communicated with Dahi and asked for him to come. Why had she not?

∞-You knew you took a risk with him. He wants your life force.-∞

∞-He will come for me wherever I hide, won't he?-∞

∞-He will if he knows where you are,-∞ Bodha turned to face her. ∞-That is why he will never know.-∞

Rohongra understood. She would be safe as long as she kept public thought to herself. ∞-Where are you taking me?-∞

∞-A safe place.-∞

∞-And what of the Hu-Mans? Those who are with me?-∞

∞-They sleep in the hold. They will join you on the planet.-∞

Rohongra released breath. Her private thoughts went to E'nov. If Most High Bodha sequestered her alone in space, it would be nice to have at least one to speak with. She had more questions, but Bodha's next thoughts stopped her.

∞-My Beings will also join you later.-∞

∞-You will return to Yon-Ya to get them? Won't that increase the chance Dahi will find me?-∞

Bodha shook his head. ∞-It only increases the chance my Beings will survive the coming conflict.-∞

Chapter 35

Mandy jumped when she heard the lock on the door to the medical center turn. She hadn't been paying attention, her mind wandering over what had happened to Phillip and what they should do now. And she worried about Francine.

Down the hallway, Francine walked slowly toward them. Her eyes were red-rimmed. Mandy had no idea how much time had passed since she'd left her or how long Doc and Aspen had been with Phillip. She lifted her arm as if to look at a watch before realizing she hadn't had one on her wrist for months.

When the door opened, she saw both Aspen and Doc wearing garbage bags, masks and gloves. Mandy moved away from them, bumping into Charlie, while Francine and Evan stepped closer.

"Okay, we've had a slight problem," Doc stated.

Evan sucked in air. His face, though, gave away no emotion.

"Something started growing inside of Phillip. We've disinfected, but we ought to take him out of the Biosphere quickly."

"What do you mean?" Francine asked.

Mandy's brain felt foggy. She heard Doc's words, but couldn't put the information together so it made sense.

"We can talk about it later. Right now Aspen and I need some clothes and then we need to move Phillip outside. Everyone needs to help."

Evan stepped back. "I don't think I can do that," he said.

Aspen reached out a hand and touched his arm. "Please, I need clothes. We need to get this done."

Evan looked away and then nodded.

"We've double bagged his body. Here are masks and gloves. Hurry so we can get changed. It'll be worse for all of us if he stays inside." Doc left them standing in the hall and returned to the medical center, closing the door between them.

"Let's get this over with," Francine said.

Evan ran off to get clothes, returning quickly. Mandy wondered briefly about the blush to Evan's cheeks and then realized he'd had to go through Aspen's underwear drawer. If things weren't so awful, Mandy would have teased him.

"Let's go," Doc's orders broke through her thoughts.

Together, minus Dagny, they pulled, carried and dragged Phillip's body through the Biosphere. Going outside was a risk, but they put on additional clothing.

"What about Charlie?" Evan asked.

Mandy dropped to a knee. "You need to stay here and behave," she told her dog. Then Mandy stood and wrapped a scarf around her nose and mouth.

Once they were all bundled, Evan handed each one a bottle of water and they opened the door.

Quickly, Mandy scanned the hills surrounding them She hadn't been outside for a few days. The air seemed clearer, cleaner somehow.

Doc led the group up the hill, walking backwards. The wind no longer blew ash so they easily found their way to the nearest turbine. Mandy briefly wondered where Dagny had gone to hide, but quickly dismissed the thought and focused on their task. The weight of what they were doing lay heavy on her chest. Grief stirred inside of her. One foot in front of the other, she thought as she struggled to keep it together, but each step seemed more difficult. It hadn't been that long since she'd lost both parents, her brother and her friends. The wedding rings around her neck felt heavy and tears blurred her vision. It seemed the trip took forever, but really was only several minutes and then they stood below the first turbine.

"Should we burn his body?" Francine asked as they hauled Phillip's body up the slight hill.

Mandy stumbled. Too late realizing the group had stopped.

"We could, but that might draw in others. I don't want us to be exposed any longer than we have to," Doc said. "We've been lucky not to have been found.

Francine breathed heavily as her body bent in half. Sweat dripped from Mandy's forehead. She was grateful they had reached the turbine.

"Almost there," Doc said.

They lifted the body bag and climbed the stairs, opened the door and then carefully lay Phillip down in the base of one of the broken turbines as far back as they could from the door.

"I'm going to miss him," Mandy choked on her words.

"Me too. He was so carin' and considerate," Aspen added.

"His silence is louder now that's he's gone. And I, I..." Tears spilled down Francine's cheeks.

"Good-bye, Phillip," Evan said.

"Thank-you," Doc whispered so quietly Mandy couldn't be sure if she heard correctly. The sullen group headed out. Mandy took one last look at her friend's body before they shut the door.

* * *

The next day Dagny tromped into the kitchen rubbing her eyes. She'd stayed up late talking with other groups, to try and get an idea of where they could go.

"Morning," she said as merrily as she could. "How did everyone sleep?"

Everyone but Phillip sat at the table with their heads down. Belatedly she remembered his death. She shouldn't have been so upbeat.

Evan glared at her. Her eyes widened as she took a seat and grabbed for a bowl and spoon. "Where have you been?" he demanded.

"Someone had to man the two-way." She shrugged.

Bolton shook his head. Even he seemed defeated.

"What happened?" Dagny gulped. "I mean, I know what happened, but I mean after . . ."

"After Phillip died, you mean?" Francine rose from the table and turned her back to the rest.

"We took him outside," Evan said.

Mandy reached over and gave her remaining cereal to Charlie. "I should go and start . . ." Mandy stood.

"Start what?" Dagny asked, still trying to have a conversation with someone.

Mandy shrugged. "I need to check the dome systems." She picked up her bowl and moved toward the kitchen. Dagny saw her wipe tears from her eyes.

Aspen coughed behind her mask and all eyes turned toward her. Her shoulders shook. "Ah'm infected," she said.

Bolton pushed himself back from the table. "Damn," he said. "If only you'd worn the mask like I told you to. I'm sure it's the spores. You were exposed."

"Do we have any medicine? I mean now that we know what killed Phillip. Don't you think we could . . . ?" Francine asked.

Bolton smiled. "Yeah, sure. I'll get her something."

"Maybe we should leave and join with one of the other groups," Dagny interjected.

Bolton faced her with his hands on his hips. "What are you talking about?"

"People are on the move. They're banding together. I heard it on the two-way. They said it's hard, but you can make it. Maybe they'd be able to . . . ," she cast a look at Aspen, "help. There's a group who'd love to have some livestock. We could bring the lambs."

With those words, Aspen's sobs grew louder. She rose and ran from the room.

"You weren't talking to those people, were you?" Evan rose from where he'd sat.

All eyes turned toward her. Dagny swallowed. "Just enough to find out where to go."

"You knew the rules." Bolton stepped closer. He looked to Francine for confirmation.

Francine lifted her shoulders and turned away. "Who cares. Right? Phillip's dead. Aspen's sick with the same stuff. So are you most likely," she told him. Dagny recoiled. "It doesn't matter." Francine left the room.

Mandy touched Charlie's head.

"I'm sorry. I wanted to help," Dagny told Evan and Bolton.

Moments later Francine stepped back into the room. "Perhaps it's not a bad idea." She shrugged. "We could leave now, before we're too weak to make it. You don't have anything to help Aspen, do you?" she challenged Bolton.

He shook his head. "Not a thing."

"I can't leave," Mandy spoke up. "My brother."

Bolton turned to her. "You stay and you might not live to see your brother even if he makes it back. I don't know where Phillip got that - stuff, but he got it somewhere in here. Francine's right. Dagny makes sense. We should leave right away."

216

Dagny heard the sound of his voice and knew he'd given up. It startled her a bit.

"Aspen isn't strong enough," Evan said. "I heard her coughing all night. She won't make it."

"Then we have to leave her," Bolton said. He dropped his head into his hands.

"What? No! You can't mean that?" Evan's voice rose. His gaze found each person. He begged them with his eyes.

"Listen, the sooner we leave the better our chances of making it before we get too ill," Francine said.

"Gather your things. We need to travel light." Dagny pulled out the list she'd compiled with the man who'd crossed the mountains. "Here's what we need." She spread the paper on the table. "I've already gathered my things."

Francine inspected it. She shook her head and Dagny saw tears litter her lower lashes. "Okay then."

Mandy shook her head. "I won't leave. I can't." Her voice broke. She gathered Charlie toward her chest and quietly sobbed into her coat.

"Me either," Evan stated. "I'm staying with Aspen. Until . . ." He looked at his shoes. "I'm staying here," he declared.

"Fine, you stay. The rest of you, gather your things together and let's go." Francine stomped out.

* * *

"I don't understand why you'd leave. It makes no sense," Mandy pleaded. They stood inside the lung beside the exterior door a few minutes later. "There's nothing better out there. Francine, you know it's a long shot you'll find your daughter. Doc, what if you get sick?" She begged them to stay and didn't care that her eyes were swollen and tears fell.

"I couldn't help Phillip even here. Besides I don't have a cough now. I'm fine," Doc said. He avoided her gaze.

"Do you all know where you're goin'?" Aspen asked. They all stayed well away from her.

Aspen told Mandy she wasn't strong enough to go traipsing across the country. Mandy didn't have the heart to tell her she wouldn't have been invited anyway. After saying good-bye to Phillip less than twelve hours ago, and now having to say good-bye to three more family, Mandy felt drained. She hugged Francine. "Don't go."

"You'll be fine without us." Francine forced a weak smile. "Or you could change your mind and come."

"I can't. Thank-you for everything." Mandy hugged the larger woman while Aspen made gulping sobbing sounds behind her.

"Do we have everything?" Doc asked.

Francine nodded. "We're heading east if you change your mind. I have a compass, but there's another on my desk."

Doc leaned close to Mandy and whispered in her ear. "And whatever happens, don't go into the medical center. I can't be sure we got rid of it all. There are body bags in the basement. Use two. All of you should wear masks. All of the time."

Aspen's sobs grew louder. Evan touched her shoulder. Mandy moved closer to Doc to hear above Aspen's crying.

"Come on. We need to get going," Dagny said.

"Aspen, I'm truly sorry," Doc said.

He looked sincere and it surprised Mandy. She felt awful. "Good-bye," she said. He hugged her, surprising her even more. "Take care of yourselves."

Francine hugged Evan and her one last time. No one came close to Aspen. "I'll miss you," Francine told them all.

The corner of Mandy's mouth turned up, but inside, her world crashed. Mandy watched the group walk out the door to see if anyone turned around. They didn't, and eventually she locked the door, and followed Aspen and Evan into the Biomes.

218

Chapter 36

∞

∞-Most High Bodha, my Being is surprised but happy to see you,-∞ Soluma-Rah acknowledged his image before her.

∞-Are our thought's protected from others?-∞

∞-Yes. You may think freely.-∞

∞-I have transported Rohongra, and the few Hu-Mans with her, to safety. Most High Elected, Yon-Ya is not safe. Dahi occupies our planet. He is a treacherous Being. How are you going to protect us?-∞

∞-Calm yourself. I have sent warnings to those Beings who surround Yon-Ya.-∞

∞-Yes, but what about Yon-Ya itself?-∞

∞-At this time, no loss of life has occurred,-∞ Soluma-Rah thought.

∞-That is not the answer I seek. Most High, will you not aid in some protection?-∞

∞-You may bring the Beings you carry on your ship to TE-Garon. We will prepare and train them for affray.-∞

∞-Most High, as you are aware, we did not have desire for affray last time and I do not choose this course for my Beings now.-∞

∞-With respect, your peace will not protect you this time from either Dahi or Ka's Beings. The two have joined forces and we have knowledge they train the Hu-Mans in their control for war. The last time Ka's force was powerful, this time he may be strong enough to defeat us all.-∞

Most High Bodha moved away from the screen, but Soluma-Rah did not lose the connection with him. She waited, her Being silent, giving him time to confer.

∞-Momur, set the course.-∞

∞-Most High Bodha, we are one.-∞

Soluma-Rah broke off the connection. Perhaps they could survive to rule over Ka and his Beings. She knew it was necessary for peace.

Chapter 37

Mandy climbed to the top of the rainforest mountain. Charlie followed close behind. She couldn't look at Evan right now. His pain over losing Aspen suffocated her. Neither Evan nor Mandy had developed any symptoms yet, but whatever killed Phillip had taken Aspen's life after one short week.

They'd followed Doc's instructions to a "T" and had laid Aspen's body next to Phillip's in a matching body bag. The smell of decomposition in the turbine overwhelmed her senses. She pushed back bile when they first opened the door. Evan stood there a long time, but eventually Mandy had to step outside. She said her good-byes quickly not wanting to invade Evan's grief. He seemed to finally realize he needed to speak up and let Aspen know how he felt about her after she fell sick and when he could no longer do anything about his love.

Now, a few hours later, Mandy couldn't make her muscles move. Exhaustion had taken over and her eyelids were heavy. Briefly she wondered if excessive CO_2 was the reason. For the week it had taken Aspen to die, they had done nothing in the dome. She hadn't checked crops, or biomes or anything except the animals that the others had left for them and only because she couldn't let them die with Aspen.

She looked up. Charlie barked. "Shush girl. I know I need to fix the tarp." Somehow one clip had slipped and a corner of the tarp that covered the rainforest roof flapped down. "But I like looking at the sky," she told Charlie. She removed the mask from her face. She didn't care if she did get sick, she needed to breathe. "Even though not a single star can be seen. Someday, I'm sure they'll reappear. I'll see them again," she said.

She wondered where Evan was. They'd entered the Biosphere together after leaving Aspen's body and then he'd quickly hurried off, to his room, she assumed. The American Bulldog growled.

Mandy noticed Charlie staring up. Her muscles tightened and she sat rigid. She had no time to get the lights. A galago jumped out of the bush to her left. Mandy giggled at her paranoia. Just a galago baby. Nothing to worry about. Charlie growled again, low in the back of her throat and then bounded after the baby a few feet. She returned to Mandy's side, sitting half way on her lap. Mandy giggled again and pushed Charlie off. She'd look up for one last time, then she'd go to the radio and check in.

A shadow covered the opening on the roof. Mandy sucked in a deep breath and held still. It was to late for her to do anything. The shadow moved. Mandy felt the hair lifting on the back of her neck and arms. She gripped Charlie around the neck and held tight. The shadow shifted again. Mandy looked away. She wondered where she could run to, where she could hide. She heard a sound and lifted her gaze. Mandy found herself staring into rapidly blinking eyes. She touched the rings on her necklace.

Acknowledgements

It takes a community to raise a child and as many people to write a novel. There are so many to thank.

Austine Etcheverry thanks her family who is her constant support.

D. Jean Quarles would like to thank her family and the supportive community of writers who have been there every step of the way. A special thanks goes to the authors at Writers On The Move and the Critique Group Formerly of Glendale, Arizona.

Austine Etcheverry was born in Sheridan, Wyoming. A wife and mother of two, she currently resides in Avondale, Arizona. A special education coach, she writes women's fiction and young adult fiction. She is a lover of animals and currently shares a home with three dogs and six cats.

D. Jean Quarles was born in Minneapolis, MN. She currently resides in Phoenix, Arizona with her husband. She is the author of the women's fiction novels; Rocky's Mountains, Fire in the Hole and Perception. Her award winning short story, The Mermaid, was published in Tales of a Sweltering City. House of Glass is the second book in The Exodus Series, a young adult science fiction series.

www.ingramcontent.com/pod-product-compliance
Lightning Source LLC
Chambersburg PA
CBHW051501170626
46811CB00002B/579